WARPED GALAXIES

ATTACK OF THE

NECRON

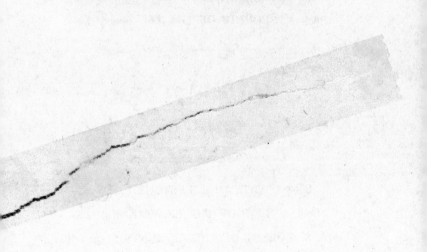

WARPED GALAXIES

REALM QUEST

WARHAMMER
ADVENTURES
STORIES FROM THE FAR FUTURE

WARPED GALAXIES

ATTACK OF THE

NECRON

CAVAN SCOTT

WARHAMMER ADVENTURES

First published in Great Britain in 2019 by
Warhammer Publishing,
Willow Road,
Nottingham, NG7 2WS, UK.

10 9 8 7 6 5 4 3 2 1

Produced by Games Workshop in Nottingham.
Cover illustration by Cole Marchetti.
Internal illustrations by Magnus Norén & Cole Marchetti.

A CIP record for this book is available from the British Library.

ISBN 13: 978 1 78496 780 2

See Warhammer Adventures on the internet at

warhammeradventures.com

Find out more about Games Workshop and the worlds of
Warhammer 40,000 and Warhammer Age of Sigmar at

games-workshop.com

Printed and bound by CPI Group (UK) Ltd, Croydon, CR0 4YY

For James.

Contents

The Imperium of the Far Future

Life in the 41st millennium is hard. Ruled by the Emperor of Mankind from his Golden Throne on Terra, humans have spread across the galaxy, inhabiting millions of planets. They have achieved so much, from space travel to robotics, and yet billions live in fear. The universe seems a dangerous place, teeming with alien horrors and dark powers. But it is also a place bristling with adventure and wonder, where battles are won and heroes are forged.

CHAPTER ONE

Intruders

Zelia Lor awoke to the sound of buzzing in her cabin. She groaned. What time was it? Her bunk creaked as she turned over, pulling her thick woollen blanket with her. Surely that couldn't be the alarm already? The shrill drone continued, flitting to and fro near the ceiling. Zelia pulled the blanket over her head, but the noise persisted. Throwing back the covers, she peered up into the gloom.

That was no alarm. There was something up there, darting back and forth.

'Hello?' Zelia called out, her voice

croaking from lack of sleep. She'd been up late last night, helping her mum catalogue artefacts in the ship's cargo bay.

A series of high-pitched chirps and whistles came from somewhere near the ceiling. Zelia reached out, feeling for the luminator switch next to her bunk. Glow-globes flickered into life, the tiny invader squealing in surprise as it was bathed in sudden light.

Zelia frowned as her eyes focused on her flighty visitor. It was a servo-sprite, one of the small winged robots that her mother used on board their planet-hopper, the *Scriptor*. The whimsical little things had been created by her mother's assistant, Mekki. They had tiny bronze bodies and spindly limbs, with probes and data-connectors for fingers and toes. Their heads were long, with wide optical-beads for eyes that gave the little automata a constant look of surprise. Mesh wings whirred on the robot's back, producing the strident buzz that had woken Zelia.

'What are you doing up there?' Zelia asked, rubbing sleep from her eyes.

The servo-sprite chattered nervously at itself. If Zelia didn't know better she would have thought the thing was agitated, but like all the robots her mother used on their expeditions servo-sprites were just machines. Elise Lor was an explorator, a scholar who travelled the length and breadth of the Imperium excavating technology from years gone by, and who often dreamed of digging up artefacts from the Dark Age of Technology, that period thousands of years ago when machines thought for themselves. Those days were long gone. Like so many things in the 41st millennium, artificial intelligence was a heresy, prohibited by order of the Eternal Emperor himself. While Mekki's creations sometimes acted as if they were alive, they were just following their programming. They were tools, nothing more. However, something must have spooked the little automaton for it to squeeze through the gap beneath her cabin door. Gooseflesh crawled over Zelia's skin. Why would a servo-sprite hide? Something was wrong.

Swinging her legs off the bunk, Zelia gasped as her bare feet touched the cold metal deck. The floors of the *Scriptor* were supposed to be heated, but like most of the systems on the ramshackle spaceship, the heating hadn't worked properly for months. The planet-hopper was old – very old – and its systems often failed faster than Mekki could fix them. But for all its glitches, the *Scriptor* had been Zelia's home since she was born. She knew every creak of the hull, every bleep of the central cogitator. The low thrum of the engines lulled her to sleep every night. They were a comfort, especially during long journeys across the Imperium, rocketing from one dig to another. It was an odd, topsy-turvy life, helping her mum uncover crashed spaceships or ancient machines on distant worlds all across the galaxy, but Zelia wouldn't have it any other way.

But now, the *Scriptor* didn't feel comforting. It felt uneasy, and Zelia had no idea why. Pulling on her jacket and bandolier, Zelia tapped the vox stitched into her sleeve. The communicator beeped, opening a channel to the flight deck.

'Mum? Are you there?'

There was no reply, neither from mum, nor Lexmechanic Erasmus, her mother's archaeological partner and an expert in galactic languages, both ancient and alien. There was no point trying to contact Mekki. Her mum's young assistant was a whizz with technology, but hardly ever spoke to Zelia, even though they were around the same age. At twelve, she was a full year older than Mekki was, but they were largely strangers, the Martian boy preferring the company of his machines.

Zelia didn't mind. If she was honest, Mekki made her a little uncomfortable. He was so intense, with his pale skin and cold grey eyes.

Still, he would know what to do with a flustered servo-sprite.

The robot bumbled around her head as she opened the cabin door. She swatted it away, but it stayed close as she stepped out into the corridor. The passageway was quiet, electro-candles spluttering along the creaky walls.

The door to her mum's cabin was ajar, and Zelia could see it was empty. For a woman who spent her life cataloguing artefacts, Elise Lor was incredibly untidy. Curios from her travels were crammed into nooks and crannies, while towers of textbooks and battered data-slates teetered on every available surface. Elise's library was spread throughout the ship, piled high along the narrow gantries. How mum ever found anything was a mystery, and yet she always seemed to be able to put her finger on any text at a moment's notice.

But where was she now? Zelia crept down the corridor, checking Erasmus's cabin, but the elderly scholar was nowhere to be seen. He wasn't in his room or on the mess deck where the *Scriptor*'s crew gathered to eat. Zelia checked the chrono-display on her vox. It was early, barely sunrise. Had mum and Erasmus gone to the dig already?

Zelia jumped at a noise from the back of the ship. Something heavy had been dropped, the deep clang echoing around the planet-hopper. That had to have come from the cargo bay, where Elise stored their most valuable discoveries. They had been on this planet, a remote hive world called Targian, for three months now, and the hold was brimming with ancient tech. Of course, the noise could just have been Mekki, checking through the previous day's finds, but somehow, she knew it wasn't. Mekki was a lot of things, but clumsy wasn't one of them. He would never drop something if he could help it. As the servo-sprite fussed around her head, Zelia picked up a heavy-looking ladle that Elise had used to slop grox stew into their bowls the night before. It wasn't much of a defence, but it would have to do.

Zelia inched towards the cargo bay, praying that she'd find Mekki on the other side of the hold's heavy doors. She paused, listening through the thick metal. There was a flurry of movement on the other side of the door, the scrape of leather against deck-plates, and then silence. Trying to ignore the increasingly frantic buzzing of the servo-sprite, Zelia stepped forwards and the doors wheezed open.

'Hello? Mekki, are you in here?'

There was no answer. The cargo bay was silent, the lights kept permanently low to protect the more valuable artefacts. She crept through the collection, tall cabinets on either side.

Something moved ahead. Her grip tightened on the ladle.

'Mekki? Seriously, this isn't funny.'

A boot crunched behind her. Zelia whirled around, swinging the ladle.

'You need to be careful,' a gruff voice said. 'You could hurt someone with that!'

Zelia cried out as thick fingers caught her wrist. They squeezed, and the metal spoon clattered to the floor.

'That's better.'

A stranger loomed over her, muscles bunched beneath a scruffy vest festooned with brightly coloured patches. His hair was styled into a lurid green mohawk, a tattoo of a large red cat leaping over his left ear. It was a Runak – a ferocious scavenger native to Targian with jagged scales instead of fur. Zelia had only seen the creatures out on the plains, but imagined they smelled better than the thug who was threatening her in her own home.

'Let go of me,' Zelia cried out, trying to pull away.

'I don't think so, Ladle-Girl,' the tattooed thug leered, before calling over his shoulder. 'You can come out. It's only a little brat.'

Brat? The thug must only have been a year or two older than Zelia. He was strong though. There was no way of breaking his grip. More strangers slipped out of the shadow – two boys, and a girl with spiked purple hair and a glowing eye-implant. They all wore similar patches on their jackets, obviously members of the same gang.

'What do you want?' Zelia squeaked, and her captor smiled, showing uneven, stained teeth.

'That's a good question.' The thug glanced around, his small, cruel eyes scanning the rusting relics on the shelves. 'We thought this place would be full of treasure, didn't we, Talen?'

The ganger behind him nodded. This one wasn't as big, but still looked like he could handle himself in a fight. His blond hair was cropped short at the sides and a small scar ran through one of his thick, dark eyebrows. He held no weapons in his gloved hands, but Zelia couldn't help but notice the snub-nosed beamer hanging next to the leather pouch on his belt.

'That's what you told us, Rizz, but it looks like a load of old junk to me.'

'Yeah, old junk,' Rizz parroted, pulling Zelia closer. 'Where's the real booty? Where've you stashed it?'

'This is all we have,' Zelia told him, glancing down at the hefty weapon Rizz held in his free hand. The ganger had fashioned a mace out of a long girder topped with a blunt slab of corroded metal.

'You like my spud-jacker?' Rizz said, brandishing the makeshift weapon. 'I call her Splitter. Do you want to know why?'

'I think I can guess,' Zelia replied.

''Cos, I split skulls with her,' he said anyway, as if she were the idiot, not him. 'Ain't that right, Talen?'

The blond-haired juve shifted
uncomfortably, glancing nervously at the
cargo bay doors. 'We should go, Rizz.
There's nothing here.'

Rizz glared at the younger kid. 'Oi. I
give the orders. Not you.'

'Then order us to get out of here.
We're wasting our time.'

Rizz swung around, nearly pulling
Zelia off her feet.

'I'll waste you in a minute,'

he growled, brandishing Splitter menacingly.

Zelia saw her chance and took it. She lashed out with her foot, kicking Rizz's shin.

'Ow!' he yelped, spinning her around so she crashed into the nearest cabinet, cogs and gears tumbling all around her. Zelia snatched a length of metal piping from the floor, but a swipe of the spud-jacker sent it flying across the cargo bay.

'Nice try,' Rizz sneered above her. 'But I'm not going to ask you again. Where's the valuable stuff? Where are you hiding it?'

'I told you,' she shouted back, gripping her aching fingers. 'This is all there is.'

'Liar,' Rizz bellowed, raising the spud-jacker high above his head. 'Splitter hates liars, and so do I.'

With a feral roar, he brought the mace crashing down.

CHAPTER TWO

The Runak Warriors

'No!' Talen yelled, barging into Rizz and throwing off the larger ganger's aim. Splitter smashed harmlessly into the deck.

'What do you think you're doing?' Rizz thundered, swinging the spud-jacker at Talen. The blond-haired boy leapt back, the club narrowly missing him. The next time he wasn't so lucky. Rizz lashed out again with the mace, catching Talen in the side. The boy crashed into a cabinet, the air knocked out of him.

'Leave him alone,' Zelia yelled.

'Stay out of this, girl,' Rizz sneered, as

the rest of the gang stepped back, too scared to interfere. 'He's gone too far this time.' He loomed over Talen, the spud-jacker held high.

Zelia looked up. The servo-sprite was still buzzing around the ceiling. She tapped the vox on her sleeve, activating a channel to the ship's central cogitator.

'Danger in cargo bay,' she shouted. 'Protect the artefacts!'

'Eh?' Rizz said, his spud-jacker frozen in mid-air. 'What's that supposed to mean?'

'You'll see,' said Zelia with a smile, as every servo-sprite Mekki had ever constructed swarmed on the cargo and descended on the gangers.

'Aaaargh!' Rizz screamed as dozens of tiny robots jabbed at him with needle-sharp data-connectors. 'Get them off me!' He tried to swat them away with Splitter but only lost his balance, crashing to the floor.

The other gangers ran into each other as they were mobbed by the servo-swarm. Even Talen was forced to throw up his arms to protect himself, but Zelia saw him grin at her before yelling at the others: 'Let's get out of here!'

They all ran, Rizz included, still swiping at the servo-sprites that yanked painfully at his mohawk.

Zelia jumped to her feet as soon as they were gone. She ran to the cogitator terminal next to the doors, activating the ship's pict-feed. Images scrolled over the display, displaying pict-casts from every corner of the ship. She scrolled through to the external feeds and watched the gang-members charge down the *Scriptor*'s ramp, servo-sprites dive-bombing the would-be raiders like fire-wasps. As soon as they were clear, she pressed a button and the ramp swung up to slam shut.

Suddenly exhausted, Zelia slumped forward, leaning heavily against the terminal. Her legs were like jelly, her breath ragged.

She tapped her vox.

'Mum? Are you there? Mum?'

Elise still didn't answer. That settled it. If her mum wasn't on the ship, and wasn't answering her vox, then there was only one place she could be.

'Ouch!' cried Talen as one of the small flying robots jabbed the back of his neck. 'You wanted us off the ship. We're off the ship.'

The automaton chattered angrily in return, and Talen couldn't help but smile. Ladle-Girl had done good. It took a lot to take on the Runak Warriors, but she had sent them packing.

Their job done, the servo-sprites flocked back to the funny little ship, disappearing into a porthole.

'Let's get back underground,' Talen shouted, but Rizz wasn't happy.

'You don't tell me what to do, Talen. Not now, not ever. We're going back onto that ship to teach that runt a lesson she'll never forget.'

The others didn't move, looking from Rizz to Talen, not sure who to follow. Talen's hand dropped down to his beamer.

Rizz snorted. 'You going to blast me, Talen? Is that it? It's funny – in all the years you've had that clipped to your belt, I've never seen you use it. You haven't got the guts. You're a coward, Guard Boy, always have been, always will be.'

Talen didn't have a chance to respond to the jibe.

A cry echoed across the vast landing-bay and he turned to see a soldier of the Astra Militarum making straight for them through the clustered space cruisers. He was wearing the Imperial Guard's standard khaki-green uniform, a long shock-stick gripped in his gloved hand, capable of delivering a charge that could stop a full-grown grox in its tracks.

'Hey!' the Guardsman shouted. 'What are you tunnel-rats doing up here?'

Rizz cursed, shooting one last venomous look at the planet-hopper before yelling: 'Scatter!'

The Warriors did as they were told, Talen included. He ducked behind a stack of crates, heading for a bolthole at the far end of the space port. He didn't bother looking back for the others. At times like this, it was every ganger for themselves, especially where Rizz was concerned.

Talen dropped to the ground at the first sound of las-fire, sliding towards a service hatch. He lifted the heavy lid to reveal a ladder. It led down to a tunnel, part of the ventilation system that pumped recycled air around the hive. He started clambering down, glancing up to see Essa lying on the floor. The purple-haired girl was out cold, stunned by the Guardsman's shock-stick. Talen swore beneath his breath. This wouldn't go well for them back at camp... and all for a planet-hopper filled with old junk. Typical Rizz.

He started to climb down, stopping only at the sound of a spluttering grav-bike. It was the girl from the planet-hopper, weaving in and out of the other ships in the space port.

'Where are you going?' he wondered aloud, before a fresh barrage of las-fire sent him hurrying down the ladder.

The Runak Warriors were just one of the many gangs that inhabited the tunnels and sewers beneath Rhal Rata, the largest of Targian's many hive-cities. They operated out of a long-forgotten storm drain, their camp in little danger of being flooded on a planet that hadn't seen a single drop of rain for decades.

The gang had been Talen's surrogate family ever since he'd run away from home three years ago. They were an untrustworthy bunch of thieves and cut-throats but had taken him in when he needed it most. That didn't mean he was going to cover himself in ganger-tattoos like Rizz. He wasn't stupid. Talen wore a Runak patch on his vest to show his allegiance, and that was good enough for him. Something about tattoos made his skin crawl. He remembered his brother proudly showing off his aquila tattoo the day he'd joined the Imperial Guard.

'What do you think, Tally?' Karl had asked. The skin around the official sigil of the Imperium was red raw, the two-headed eagle forever branded into his brother's arm.

'Looks great,' he'd lied, even though it made him feel sick, and Karl had ruffled his hair.

'You'll have one of your own, one day,' Karl promised him.

Not likely, Talen had thought. Everyone was so sure that Talen was going to follow in Karl's footsteps. It was a family tradition, after all. Their father, Tyrian Stormweaver, had trained generations of Imperial Guardsmen. It was only natural that his sons would go into the service.

'It's your duty, boy,' he would growl at his younger son. 'It'll make a man of you. Throne knows, something has to...'

Talen wondered what his dad would think of him now. His son, the tunnel-rat...

The Runak camp was unnaturally quiet when Talen clambered into the drain. He sighed. This could only mean one thing. Everyone had already gathered in Onak's Great Hall. Rizz would have already taken centre stage, telling their leader what had happened... or at least, his side of the story. What was the betting that Talen was getting blamed for Essa's capture?

In reality, the so-called Great Hall was a burned-out troop carrier. Talen had no idea how it had got down here. Legend said that Onak's father had stripped the transport down piece by piece and floated it through the sewers. It had been rebuilt in pride of place at the centre of the drain, the other shacks and tents clustered around its blackened hull. By all accounts, Onak's father had been a force to be reckoned with, a legacy his daughter traded on to this day. She was as lazy as he had been brave, but the rest of the gang worshipped the ground she slouched on, especially when she had a stubcannon in hand. She was playing with the weapon now as she lounged on her throne, another relic of her father's reign, fashioned from a gunship ejector seat. The rest of the Warriors huddled around the walls listening to Rizz, who was gesturing wildly with his spud-jacker in the middle of the Great Hall.

'It's all Talen's fault,' he claimed. 'You should have seen the treasures inside that ship. They were worth a fortune, but Talen attacked me before I could take what was rightfully mine.'

'"Mine"?' Onak drawled, raising a pierced eyebrow.

Rizz bowed low to cover his mistake. 'Yours, leader.'

'He's a liar!' Every face turned to watch Talen as he strode into the assembly. 'There was nothing worth stealing on that crate, just a load of broken machines.'

'Then why did you attack me?' Rizz spat back.

'A good question,' Onak agreed from her throne.

'Because our brave Champion was about to flatten an unarmed girl.'

Rizz growled. 'She deserved it.'

'Why? Because she kicked you in the shin?' Talen stuck out his bottom lip. 'Poor baby.'

'Is that what happened, Champion?' Onak asked, barely disguising the disdain in her voice.

Rizz whirled around to face the throne. 'She had robots,' he lied, desperate to save face. 'Huge, hulking robots, armed to their metallic teeth.'

Talen laughed out loud. 'You're kidding. Is that really what you're going with?' Talen turned to address their leader. 'Oh, Rizz is a champion all right – a champion of barefaced lies. There *were* robots, but they were barely bigger than my hand.'

Rizz's face had gone as red as his tattoo. 'There were hundreds of them!'

'Three, maybe four dozen,' Talen countered. 'They were annoying, but hardly dangerous.'

'Says the one who told us to run!'

'Only because we were wasting our time. You said there was treasure on the ship, but it was a load of rubbish, just like you.'

'What?' Rizz bellowed.

'And now Essa is in the Guardhouse… because of Rizz, not me…' Talen jutted out his jaw. 'He doesn't deserve to be our Champion.'

'Take that back,' Rizz spat, brandishing his spud-jacker, 'or I'll show you how Splitter got her name!'

Talen held his ground. 'I'd like to see you try.'

'You're not the only one,' Onak said,

licking her lips as she sat up in her chair. 'Your honour has been questioned, Champion. What are you going to do about it?'

'I'll kill 'im!' Rizz roared, charging at Talen. A cheer went up from the assembled throng, the Warriors always ready to watch a good scrap, but Talen was ready for his opponent. He snatched his beamer from its holster and aimed it straight at Rizz. The Champion swung Splitter in an arc, easily knocking the beamer from Talen's grip... just as he'd been expecting.

Talen shoulder-barged Rizz, knocking the Champion off his feet. Rizz landed on his face, Splitter thudding to the floor.

Talen dropped on his rival, fists flying. The reason Rizz had never seen Talen using the beamer was that it didn't work. Talen had stolen it from his dad's barracks on the day he'd run away from home. It was a family heirloom, an antique passed down from one generation to the next. It had always been for show, unlike his fists. Talen was a brawler, whereas Rizz was nothing more than a bully. The so-called Champion had managed to fool Onak for years, but not any more. Talen would show the entire gang how much of a coward their Champion actually was.

He pummelled Rizz, but the Champion managed to kick up with his boot, catching Talen in the chest. Talen stumbled into the baying crowd and was immediately shoved back towards Rizz by at least three overexcited onlookers. That was exactly what he wanted. He pretended to tumble forward, dropping into a roll that led him straight to Splitter. He jumped up, the spud-jacker now in his hands, and swiped at Rizz. The Champion threw himself out of the way to avoid getting clobbered by his own weapon, and lost balance, landing awkwardly at Onak's feet. Talen brought the spud-jacker down, inches from Rizz's head. A gasp went up around the Great Hall, but Talen had no intention of striking the Champion. He just wanted Rizz to beg for his life, anything to show his true colours.

'Do you submit?' he yelled at the Champion as he brought the spud-jacker down on the other side of Rizz's head. 'Do you give in?'

He lifted the weapon for a third and final strike, and Rizz looked up, grinning horribly.

'Backlash!' the Champion shouted.

Electricity crackled from a powercell hidden in the spud-jacker's shaft. The energy surged into Talen's body, every muscle cramping. With a strangled cry, he crumpled to the floor, dropping the weapon.

All around them, the Warriors were chanting Rizz's name, urging their Champion to finish the job. Grinning with triumph, Rizz recovered his spud-jacker and held it high above his head like a trophy, bellowing in triumph. With his name ringing in everyone's ears, he turned to Talen and lifted the bulky weapon for the final time, ready to deliver a killer blow.

'And this,' Rizz snarled, spit flying from his lips, 'is why I am Champion, and you are *nothing*!'

CHAPTER THREE

The Siren

A siren blared through the Great Hall.
Even Rizz looked around in surprise,
forgetting that he was about to flatten
his rival once and for all.

'What's that?' he asked, as Onak rose
to her feet.

'I don't believe it,' the leader said. 'It
can't be.'

'Can't be what?' Talen stammered,
still barely able to move. He'd heard
plenty of alarms in his time, mainly
from breaking into the hive's many
manufactoria and foundries, but nothing
like this. If the other alerts were like
the annoying buzzing of flies, this one

was like the roar of a lion. So loud. So urgent.

'Onak?' Rizz said, turning to their leader.

The colour had drained beneath the tattoos that smothered her face.

'I haven't heard that noise for years,' she stammered in reply, 'and even then, it was a false alarm.'

'But what does it mean?' Talen asked, struggling back to his feet.

Onak met his confused gaze, and Talen saw real fear in her eyes.

'Invasion,' she said bluntly. 'The hive is under attack.'

Zelia loved getting out of the hive. She had never been one for cities, especially the gigantic towers of the hive worlds, rising like jagged spikes from blighted landscapes all across the Imperium. Nothing about them was natural, from the rich living in luxury in the cloud-drenched spires to the poor scraping an unbearable existence in the squalid depths of the undercity.

She hated the stink of recycled air, and never feeling the heat of the sun against her skin. She had spent so much of her life outdoors, braving the elements on dozens of worlds across the Imperium. Out here, she felt alive. Out here, she felt free.

Zelia glanced back at Rhal Rata, rising high into the sky behind her. A siren blared out of the hive. What *was* that?

It took twenty minutes or so to reach the dig, her grav-bike spluttering as it skimmed over the wasteland. Her mum had set up camp in the shadow of ancient dust-blasted ruins. Dome-shaped tents huddled together, surrounded by crates ready to be transported back to the *Scriptor*.

Her mum's skimmer sat near the largest tent, but there was no sign of Elise and the others. Zelia pulled on her brakes, expecting the bike to slow. Instead, its decrepit anti-grav generator backfired, smoke billowing from the suspensors. Zelia cried out as the bike dipped, its nose striking the ground. She was thrown from her seat as the bike pinwheeled through the air. Bike and rider crashed into the dirt at the same time, sending up a plume of dust.

'Zelia?'

Elise Lor raced from the main tent, making straight for her daughter. 'Are you all right?'

There was no mistaking that Zelia

and Elise were related. They had the same dark skin and mops of unmanageable black hair piled high on their heads.

A pale-skinned boy barrelled out of the tent behind Elise.

'What have you done?' he demanded as he raced over to the smoking grav-bike.

'No, that's fine, Mekki,' Zelia muttered as Elise helped her up. 'You just worry about the bike. It's not like I nearly broke my neck, or anything.'

Elise's assistant was already examining the downed vehicle, completely oblivious to Zelia's sarcasm. He was tall and lanky, his long limbs draped in the flowing red robes of his people. Like all Martians he had a natural affinity for machines and was always tinkering with the archeotech unearthed by Elise's digs. According to Lexmechanic Erasmus, the people of Mars worshipped technology itself, and communicated with the spirits they believed inhabited all machines. Zelia wasn't sure if she believed in the existence of machine-spirits herself but knew that Mekki preferred the company of gadgets and gizmos to other humans. He even looked a bit like a machine, thanks to the exo-frame that helped him move his withered right arm. Mekki had apparently built the bionic cuff himself when he was only three years old.

As she watched, he pulled open a panel to access the bike's engine and flicked down a number of the magnifying lenses he wore on a band around his head. He went straight to work, assisted by a pair of servo-sprites that fetched tools for him from the large pack he wore on his back.

'Are you here because of the siren?' Elise asked, checking her daughter for injuries.

'No,' Zelia said, wincing as her mum brushed a graze on her cheek. 'Although, that *is* freaky.'

'Then what are you doing out of bed? I thought you deserved a lie-in after working so hard last night.'

Zelia told her about the break-in and the gangers in the hold and Elise's eyes went wide.

'What?'

She turned and stomped into the main dome, Zelia limping slightly as she tried to keep up. A silver-haired man was hunched over an antique vox in the corner of the tent, twisting knobs on the side of the dented unit as he tried to find a signal.

'Erasmus,' Elise began, her anger barely in check, 'did you lock the hatch when we left this morning?'

The man looked up in puzzlement. 'Hatch?'

'On the *Scriptor*. Zelia was attacked by gangers in our own cargo bay.'

Erasmus got up from the vox and hurried over. 'By the Emperor... Are you all right, my dear?'

'She's fine,' Elise snapped, answering

for Zelia. 'But you have to be more careful. You know how dangerous the hive can be.'

The lexmechanic scratched his cheek, stubble rasping against his fingers. 'I truly am sorry. I... I just wanted to get to the dig.'

He looked up, distracted by the siren that was still wailing across the wastelands.

'I don't like that,' he stammered, pointing in the direction of the hive. 'Not one bit.'

He scuttled back to the vox and grabbed a headset, pressing a vox-caster to his ear. 'I'm trying to find out what's happening back there, but there's a lot of chatter.'

His face suddenly went as white as his thinning hair.

'Erasmus?' Elise asked.

He leapt up from the vox without explaining. 'We need to get everything back to the *Scriptor*... now.'

'Why?' Elise asked, following Erasmus outside.

'Oh no,' he whimpered. 'It's already begun.'

Zelia shielded her eyes against the sun. There were dots on the horizon, moving in quickly. Frowning, she pulled her omniscope from her bandolier and peered through the lens.

'They're ships,' she said, as the dots swam into focus.

'What kind of ships?' Elise asked.

'I don't know. I've never seen anything like them.'

That was true enough. The ships were shaped like crescents, their dark green wings curling forward like the jaws of a nighthawk beetle. Strange sigils glowed green along the ships' sides, as did the cannons that jutted out beneath the cockpits. They were moving at speed, the unnatural howl of their engines competing with the blare of the siren.

Zelia tried to zoom in on the nearest fighter. It looked like there was a pilot sitting in the open cockpit but she couldn't quite make it out.

'Identification?' she asked out loud.

'Unknown,' the scope's inbuilt cogitator replied in a clipped version of her mum's voice.

'Let me see,' Erasmus said, snatching the scope from her hands.

'Hey! Careful!' The omniscope had been a present from Elise. Her mum had dug it up on Mannia-4, and had

Mekki fix the ancient cogitator, using her own voice print as a joke.

'You can finally order me around, Zelia... if you dare.'

No one was laughing now. Erasmus let out a whimper as he adjusted the scope, seeing the bizarre craft for himself.

'What are they, Erasmus?' Elise asked.

'Don't you recognise the sound?' he said, shoving the scope into Elise's hands and rushing back into the tent.

'No,' Elise said, shaking her head as she looked through the device. That's not possible. They're extinct.'

'Extinct?' Zelia asked.

'That's what we thought,' Erasmus shouted from inside the dome. 'But what if we were wrong?'

'Mum?' Zelia asked, her voice wavering. 'What are they?'

Elise crouched down in front of Zelia and gave her the scope.

'You'll need to be brave, sweetheart. Really brave. We all will.'

'You're scaring me, mum.'

'I'm scared too, baby, and for good reason.'

Behind her, the first wave of fighters had already reached the hive. How had they moved so fast? The strange craft opened fire, their cannons spitting bolts of emerald energy.

'They're called the Necrons,' Elise said, 'and they won't rest until they've destroyed every living thing on this planet.'

CHAPTER FOUR

The Necrons

The strange green energy punched deep into the hive, fire blossoming wherever it struck. It was more like lightning than las-fire, crackling from the Necron cannons. But the invaders weren't just targeting the city. More of the emerald beams were carving deep canyons into the ground beyond the hive, a fog of dust and rubble clouding the horizon.

'Grab as much as you can,' Elise said, making for the tent. 'Mekki, how's that grav-bike looking?'

The Martian boy shook his head. 'The motivators are fused. It is going to take time to repair.'

'We haven't time,' Erasmus said, charging out of the tent, his arms brimming with artefacts.

Elise grabbed one of the containers stacked beside the dome. 'We can use my skimmer. Zelia, take this.'

She passed the heavy container to Zelia, who struggled over to the hover-sled. Before long the skimmer was piled high with artefacts.

'We won't be able to take much more, mum,' Zelia said as Elise appeared with even more relics.

'We should go,' Erasmus agreed, slinging a leather satchel over his shoulder.

Elise hesitated, looking back at the containers still scattered around the camp. 'You're probably right, but the specimens...'

'There will be other digs, Elise,' the lexmechanic told her, clambering into the skimmer. 'We've already waited too long.'

The ground shook, and Zelia stumbled.

That had been the third earth tremor in as many minutes.

Elise leapt onto the skimmer. 'Zelia... Mekki... get on.'

Zelia was about to follow her mum onto the craft when she spotted something in the distance. The ground between them and the hive was changing colour, a dark stain sweeping out across the plain.

She opened the scope and zoomed in, letting out a gasp. A vast swarm of metallic insects was scurrying towards them on sharp, multijointed legs.

"'And lo, the Necron scarabs thronged,'" an ashen-faced Erasmus muttered from the back of the skimmer, "'devouring everything in sight.'"

'Not helpful, Erasmus,' Elise said, reaching a hand down to help Zelia onto the hover-sled.

'What's he talking about?' Zelia asked, climbing on board.

'It's nothing,' Elise said, but Zelia

could tell she was lying. 'Just a fragment of text from the Rakosan Scrolls...' Her eyes went wide. 'Oh, no.'

'What?'

Elise jumped from the skimmer and ran back to the main dome. 'I forgot my data-slate. It has all my notes. Start her up, Zelia.'

Zelia shuffled over to the driver's seat and started the engine. The skimmer's anti-grav generators whirred and the hover-sled rose unsteadily into the air to hang a metre from the ground.

'Mum, come on!' she yelled across the camp.

'What is that?' Mekki asked, pointing from where he had positioned himself among the tech.

Zelia followed his gaze to see hover-chariots racing towards them. Each looked like a floating green throne, armed to the teeth with powerful cannons. Metallic figures were hunched over the controls, looking for all the world like mechanical skeletons.

'Are those robots?' Zelia asked.

'No,' Erasmus replied. 'Those are the Necrons. They're alive... in a manner of speaking.'

'But artificial intelligence is prohibited,' Mekki said, sounding appalled.

'There's nothing artificial about it,' the lexmechanic replied, before glancing back at the tent. 'Where *is* Elise?'

Zelia's mum darted out of the dome, a data-slate clasped in her hand. 'Sorry. I couldn't leave this behind. It–'

The nearest Necron fired, green lightning lancing across the camp to slam into the ancient ruin. Fragments of rock flew everywhere, the shock wave knocking Elise from her feet.

'Mum!'

Elise scrambled up and vaulted into the seat beside Zelia.

'I'm all right. Go, go!'

Zelia opened the throttle, expecting the skimmer to shoot forwards.

It didn't move. She stamped on the accelerator, but it still didn't respond.

'Mekki,' Elise yelled. 'What's wrong with it?"

The Martian leapt from the skimmer and peered into the engine, lenses flicking down in front of his eyes. 'There is no power to the forward thrusters,' he reported, his voice unwavering. 'I can fix it.'

'Then make it quick,' Erasmus snapped.

A blast of Necron energy atomised the main tent. Fragments of canvas settled

all around like burning flakes of snow.

The Necrons were almost upon them. Their faces were like steel skulls, green eyes glowing malevolently beneath scowling brows.

Another bolt of luminous energy crackled towards them, heading straight for the skimmer.

'Everyone out,' Zelia screamed, but it was already too late.

CHAPTER FIVE

Space Marines

The lightning never found its target. A huge teardrop-shaped pod crashed down in front of them, blocking the Necron energy with its riveted metal sides. Heavy ramps slammed down, sending up a fresh cloud of dust. Zelia coughed, unable to see, but there was no mistaking the heavy stomp of boots or the clanking of battle-ravaged armour. Zelia had never seen one up close but knew exactly who the arrivals were. Everyone did. They were living legends, sworn protectors of humanity against the horrors of the universe. They were war made flesh.

They were Space Marines.

The dust settled and Zelia found
herself looking up at an armoured
giant almost three times her height, its
imposing helm staring right at her.

'Get away from here,' the Space
Marine rumbled in a voice so deep that
she could feel it in her bones. 'Now!'

She could barely move, let alone
respond. She had seen pictures of the
Ultramarines, the blue armour familiar

from hundreds of tattered tapestries and stained-glass viewports, but to see one face-to-face? That was both an honour and a curse. Those who found themselves on the battlegrounds of the Adeptus Astartes very rarely survived to tell the tale.

As she gaped, the Space Marine joined his brothers, charging into battle, his whirring chainsword held high. He brought the mighty weapon down, slicing straight through the nearest Necron battle-skimmer. The alien's cannon exploded in a blaze of green light. By the time the glare faded, the Space Marine had already moved on to its next target, along with the rest of his squad.

'Mekki?' Elise yelled down at the Martian. 'Any time soon would be good!'

'Working on it,' the Martian boy said, up to his elbows in cables.

Zelia looked to where the scarabs had reached her abandoned anti-grav bike. The metal insects scuttled over its chassis, jaws chattering. One minute the grav-bike was there, and the next it had gone. The scarabs had dismantled it in seconds, devouring every single part. Now she understood what the old scroll had meant. Worst of all, they'd be next if they didn't get the skimmer moving.

'Mekki…'

'Yes,' the Martian snapped back. 'I know.'

Zelia peered over the side. Mekki's right hand was pressed against a circuit board, the tiny haptic implants on his fingertips plugging into the skimmer's cogitator. His eyes were closed, his lips moving as if in prayer as the strange metal strips he called his 'electoos' glowed eerily on his arms and head. With a rattle, the skimmer shook. Mekki disengaged his fingers and opened his eyes, looking straight at her.

'Try it now, Zelia Lor.'

She revved the engine and the skimmer jolted forwards.

'You did it,' Elise cheered, helping Mekki onto the back of the skimmer.

'Of course,' he said plainly, his servo-sprites dropping onto his shoulders. There was no arrogance in his voice. It was merely a statement of fact.

Zelia opened the throttle and the skimmer shot forwards. She weaved the craft through the battling Space Marines, avoiding both Necron lightning and Space Marine artillery.

'Get us back to the *Scriptor*,' Elise shouted. 'We're getting off this planet.'

By the look of it, they weren't the only ones. The hive was still under attack, much of the gigantic spike ablaze, and ships of all sizes were blasting off from the space port located halfway up the towering structure. The evacuation of Targian had begun.

A Necron scarab leapt up onto the front of the skimmer and sank its pointed teeth into the metal.

'Oh no you don't,' cried Elise, grabbing

an ancient generator coil from a crate
of artefacts. She lobbed the artefact
at the scarab, knocking the one-eyed
bug from the skimmer. The paint had
blistered where it had plunged its fangs
into the metalwork, smoke curling from
two perfectly round holes.

Another scarab appeared beside Zelia.
She cried out in alarm and knocked it
from the side of the skimmer before
it could take a bite. The hover-sled
lurched to the right as she took her

eyes from the controls. She straightened up but could hear the scamper of tiny legs on the bottom of the chassis.

'We're going to be smothered by those things in a minute,' she yelled.

Mekki tapped the screen he kept cuffed to his left wrist. 'Go up,' he told her.

'What do you mean?'

'What I said. Fly.'

She twisted in her seat. 'Mekki – what are you talking about? This is a skimmer, not an aircraft.'

The ghost of a smile played over his pale lips. 'Not any more. I gave the anti-grav generator ideas above its station. Look.'

Leaning across her, he grabbed the controls.

'Hey!'

Mekki pulled back sharply on the steering wheel, and the skimmer soared into the sky. Unwilling to give up on their prize, some of the scarabs took to the air, razor-sharp wings sprouting from their glistening exoskeletons, but the skimmer was moving too fast, even for them.

Zelia laughed out loud. Mekki was a bit weird, but he was also brilliant.

'We will not be able to stay up here for long,' he told her gravely, 'but the powercell should last until we get back to the *Scriptor*.'

The skimmer suddenly dipped, dropping like a stone before levelling out again.

'You sure about that?' she gasped.

'It's not the skimmer,' Erasmus cried out as a Necron crawled onto the back of the hover-sled. The gruesome skeleton grabbed Erasmus's satchel strap and pulled, trying to yank the lexmechanic out of the skimmer. 'Help me!'

Mekki leant over, attempting to pry the alien's fingers from the bag, while the servo-sprites dive-bombed the skull-faced attacker.

'It won't let go!' Erasmus wailed.

'Hang on!' Zelia said. She had problems of her own. One of the crescent-shaped fighters had spotted them and was swooping down to intercept. Zelia swerved as the gunship fired, the crackling energy missing them by inches.

The Necron fighter threw itself into a tight turn, coming around for a fresh attack. Zelia gunned the engine but would never be able to outrun the alien ship. Its Necron pilot locked on to her and prepared to fire...

Before exploding into a ball of flaming shrapnel.

Zelia looked up to see an aquila shining bright on the nose of a thundering blue aircraft. Bristling with missile launchers and plasma cannons, the heavily armoured fighter was chunky and compact. It looked far too heavy for its hooked wings, each emblazoned with the silver U-shaped insignia that the Ultramarines wore on their shoulder pads. And yet, despite its obvious heft, the gunship turned and twisted in the air with ease, the Space Marine at the controls already targeting another Necron ship.

Behind her, Erasmus screamed. The Necron nearly had him out of the skimmer.

'Just let go of the bag,' Elise shouted.

'No,' Erasmus said. 'I can't.'

Zelia looked up and saw the Space Marine throw his gunship into a barrel roll, corkscrewing through the air. Suddenly, she knew what to do.

'Hold on to something,' she barked.

'Why?' Elise asked.

'Just do it!'

Zelia jerked the controls to the right. The skimmer went into a spin, its cargo of ancient artefacts spraying out like sparks from the whirling firecrackers that her mother launched each and every Ascension Day. The relics tumbled to the ground, where they were instantly devoured by the sea of scarabs below. Mekki grabbed hold of Erasmus as the Necron lost its grip and plunged to the ground with them.

Wrestling with the controls, Zelia levelled out the now empty skimmer.

'Is everyone all right?'

'Yes,' Erasmus stammered. 'Thanks to you.'

'Sorry about your artefacts, mum.'

Elise squeezed her daughter's arm. 'Are you kidding? That was *incredible!*'

'All thanks to Mekki's tinkering,' she said, glancing back at the Martian. He was sitting looking straight ahead. Were those tears in his eyes? Then she realised why. Only one of the servo-sprites was clinging to his robes. The other must have gone down with the Necron.

Zelia faced front, staring through the skimmer's plastek windscreen. There wasn't time to grieve for a robot, no matter how attached Mekki was to his creations. They needed to get back to the *Scriptor* before another Necron tried to bring them down. She had only just managed to pull off that manoeuvre without losing control. Next time she might not be so lucky.

CHAPTER SIX

Into Battle

Talen felt as if he knew every inch of
the tunnels beneath Rhal Rata. That
was impossible, of course. The world
beneath the city was nearly as big as
the one above. But it had been his
home for the last three years.

He had fallen in with the Runak
Warriors within weeks of running away
from home. It was impossible to survive
in the underhive without joining a
gang. He didn't like everything about
the Warriors – Rizz, included – but
they'd kept him safe... up to now.

'Keep moving,' Rizz hissed behind
him. They were scrambling along a

ventilation shaft on their hands and knees, splashing through Throne knew what. Talen had never been so glad for the pads he wore around his knees. He didn't want to think what lurked in the stagnant water that pooled in the pipes, which snaked through the hive at all levels.

'What do you think I'm doing?' he snapped back, tempted to slip and 'accidentally' boot Rizz in his stupid, tattooed face.

There was another explosion above them. Dust tumbled from cracks in the pipe. They had travelled back up to the middle section of the tower, using an abandoned maintenance lift that the Warriors used to reach the space port, and with it the rich pickings of the starfarers who used the dock. Up here, the noise of battle was louder than ever.

'Who do you think it is?' Rizz stammered. His voice was smaller than usual.

Talen didn't hesitate with his reply. 'Xenos.'

'Aliens?' Rizz squeaked. 'Are you sure?'

'What else would it be?'

Talen had heard about aliens all his life. His dad didn't believe in telling kids fairy stories.

They need to know what the universe is really like,' the old soldier used to tell Talen's long-suffering mum. Talen and Karl went to bed every night with horror stories ringing in their ears, tales of Greenskins and Tyranids, Eldar and T'au. Major Tyrian Stormweaver didn't skimp on the details. He wanted his sons to be terrified of anything that wasn't human.

He wanted them ready to fight.

'Aliens are scum, boys, never forget that. You can't trust them. They certainly don't trust us. They live only to destroy... to corrupt. That's why I joined the Imperial Guard, as did my father before me. That's why you'll join too. It's the duty of every Stormweaver

to take up arms against the xenos threat.'

They came to a T-junction in the shaft.

'Go left,' Rizz told him.

'Not likely,' Talen replied, heading right. 'That leads to the barracks.'

'So? There'll be weapons there.'

'Yeah, and there'll be fighting too. The invaders are bound to target the Guardhouse first.' Talen's chest tightened. Would his dad be there, facing the enemy, lasgun in hand? 'Besides, you've got Splitter, haven't you?'

Rizz's spud-jacker was strapped to the Champion's back and had been scraping along the pipe ever since they broke camp.

They came to a ladder, which headed up to a maintenance hatch. The hinges squealed as Talen opened it, but no one came to investigate. The Rhal Ratans had bigger concerns than a couple of gangers.

* * *

They emerged in a dingy back alley near Space Port Market on the middle levels. Onak's orders had been clear.

'It'll be chaos up top. Grab whatever you can – food, supplies, weapons – and get back down here. We'll be safe in the camp.'

Talen didn't believe that for a minute, but knew what happened if you disobeyed Onak. She had been right about one thing, though – the streets *were* in chaos. The rattle of autocannons was everywhere, accompanied by screams and the concussive blasts of frag grenades.

'Come on,' said Rizz, drawing Splitter and barging past Talen. 'I don't want to be up here for long.'

Rizz stalked out of the alley and crossed the usually busy thoroughfare. The market had been abandoned, most of the stalls already looted by rival gangs. The market catered mainly for the space port and the manufactoria of the middle levels, a heady mix of off-worlders and local labourers. The place reeked of oil and sweat, an unnatural fog hanging in the air.

Rizz's spud-jacker smashed against the metal shutters of a workshop on the other side of the street. Talen rushed over to him. 'What are you doing?'

'This is old Hinkins's place. You know, the toolsmith? I saw him fixing an old lascutter the other day. Bet he's left it behind. You can do some serious damage with a lascutter.'

A blast ripped around the corner of the street, scattering debris across the road.

'What was that?' Rizz said, forgetting all about his prize.

His answer came as three Guardsmen backed across the end of the street, firing at an unseen enemy.

Talen grabbed Rizz's arm. 'We need to go.'

Green energy lanced through the air and the soldiers were turned to dust. Rizz froze where he stood, still gripping

Splitter, terrified out of his wits. Talen
went to leave him, but then stopped
himself. Rizz was a pain in the nether
regions, but he didn't deserve to end up
like those Guardsmen.

He ran back and pulled Rizz towards
the maintenance hatch. 'Come on!'

Another explosion knocked them both
off their feet. Talen hit the ground
hard, only narrowly avoiding being
crushed by Splitter, which clattered to
the floor beside him. He looked up, ears
ringing, and saw three figures stalking
through the dust and smoke.

They walked with hunched shoulders,
their skeletal limbs clanking as they
advanced on their enemy. Their eyes
glowed green, as bright as the strange
alien glyphs that gleamed at the centre
of exposed ribcages.

'Talen! Help me!'

Talen looked in the direction of the
frightened voice. Rizz was pinned to
the ground beneath a massive slab
of masonry. Talen ran to him and

attempted to pull him free. When that
didn't work, he tried to lift the huge
chunk of rockcrete from the Champion's
body. It was far too heavy.

'Do something!' Rizz whined.

At the end of the street, the Astra
Militarum were fighting back, las-fire
bouncing harmlessly from the metal
invaders' gaunt bodies. The aliens
returned fire with the large energy
blasters they wielded in their clawed

hands. Talen didn't want to see the result, not again. He looked around, seeing Splitter lying forgotten on the floor.

'You better not shock me again,' he warned, snatching up the spud-jacker. The weapon was already over his head as he turned towards the trapped Champion.

'No! What are you doing?' Rizz cried out, as Talen brought Splitter down, pummelling the unmovable chunk of debris.

'I thought you were going to hit me,' Rizz squeaked as Talen slammed the rock over and over again, cracks spider-webbing from each blow.

'Don't tempt me. Just hold still.'

At the end of the street, one of the aliens turned towards the sound of metal against rockcrete.

'Hurry up,' Rizz pleaded, not taking his eyes from the metal monster. The skeleton turned and strode towards them.

Talen roared with frustration as he brought the spud-jacker down one last time, splitting the rockcrete in two. He rammed the end of the staff into the crack, prising the two halves apart so Rizz could wriggle out.

The alien raised its weapon.

'Give me that,' Rizz said, clambering to his feet and grabbing Splitter. He shoved against Talen, knocking him over. Talen hit the ground hard, shards of rockcrete digging into his back. Rizz was already running for the ventilation shaft, leaving Talen for dead. The alien fired, green energy arcing towards Rizz. The beam hit the Champion between the shoulder blades and in a flash, Rizz was gone. Splitter clattered to the ground, its shaft smoking from where Rizz had gripped it mere seconds

before.

The alien swung its blaster around to face Talen. For a moment, Talen couldn't do anything. He couldn't run. He couldn't even breathe. He just stared down the barrel of the alien's glowing cannon.

A frag grenade bounced down the street before the Necron could fire, coming to rest by the invader's skeletal feet. The Necron looked down, and...

BOOM!

Talen threw up his hand to protect himself from the sudden flash, the pungent smoke making him gag. When he looked up, the alien's metal limbs were scattered across the floor, and an Imperial Guardswoman was yelling at him from the end of the road.

'What are you waiting for, kid?' she

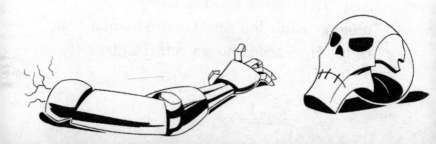

shouted. 'Get out of here before—'

The woman's voice trailed off. She was staring down to where the alien had been, eyes wide with disbelief. The skeleton's twisted limbs were crawling back towards each other, the hideous body reforming piece by piece. Within seconds it was standing tall, missing only its ghastly head. It reached down, finding the silver skull next to its discarded cannon. Its fingers clanked on the metal as it returned the head to its neck. There was a sharp click and its sunken eyes blazed green once more.

Sparks bounced off the reanimated monster as the Guard opened fire at point-blank range.

'Get to the space port,' she yelled at Talen. 'Get on a ship.'

Talen ran, only stopping to snatch up Splitter. The spud-jacker was still warm to the touch.

He could have headed back underground, but the Guardswoman was right. He needed to get off Targian. He needed to escape. Those things weren't going to stop until everyone was dead and gone.

The landing bay was in turmoil, starships already blasting off. Everywhere he looked, he could see enterprising captains offering safe passage from Targian – for the right price, of course. Talen snorted. Even now, when the world was falling around their ears, people were trying to make money.

There was only one snag – he hadn't an Imperial credit to his name.

Ahead of him, an old man struggled towards a large voidship. It was Hinkins, the toolsmith, lugging a heavy box. The oldling tripped and fell, tools spilling everywhere. Swinging Splitter onto his back, Talen ran over to help.

'Leave that alone,' Hinkins snapped as Talen grabbed a power hammer from the ground.

'I can help,' he insisted, dropping the hammer back into the old man's box.

'Just take me with you. Please.'

Hinkins looked into Talen's eyes, then down to the Runak patch on his jacket.

'I'm not with them any more,' Talen said quickly, his decision made. 'I just want to get away.'

'You and everyone else.' The old man hesitated, before shoving the box into the ganger's arms. 'I'm leaving on the *Mercator*,' he said, nodding towards the voidship. 'You can come if you carry my tools...'

'Thank you,' Talen said, as Hinkins hobbled on. 'I won't let you down.'

'You better not,' the toolsmith said. 'Come on. Shake a leg. From what I hear about her, Captain Klennon won't wait for long.'

CHAPTER SEVEN

Escape

'Going down!' Zelia screamed as the skimmer's engine finally died. The hover-sled plunged into a nosedive and carved a path through the scarabs that had crawled up the walls of the hive to scurry into the space port.

'Out!' Elise barked as the Necron scavengers overran the downed skimmer. Zelia threw herself from the doomed hover-sled and had to dodge the las-beams of Guardsmen trying to blast as many of the metallic beetles as they could.

'Are you all right?' Elise asked as the soldiers herded them towards the landing bays.

Zelia nodded, catching her breath. 'Just need to work on my landings.'

'We're never going to make it to the *Scriptor*,' Erasmus said, still clutching his satchel.

The lexmechanic had a point. Zelia had never seen such turmoil. People were trampling over each other to get to the ships, their cries drowned out by the engines of dozens of star cruisers trying to take off at once. Above them, two shuttles collided in mid-air, crashing back to the ground as would-be evacuees jumped out of the way of the burning wrecks.

Elise grabbed Zelia's hand and dragged her through the crowd, Mekki and Erasmus following close behind. No one was looking where they were going. Zelia lost grip of her mum's hand and was about to shout after her when screams broke out on the other side of the space port, near the market. As one, the heaving mass of people turned and ran. A short stubby man with bare hairy feet barged into Zelia, knocking her to the floor. She screamed, curling into a ball to stop herself being crushed. Hands grabbed her, pulling her up. It was Mekki, his remaining servo-sprite buzzing above the stampeding crowd.

'Why are people running?' she asked, and then heard the telltale sound of crackling lightning. She twisted around to see a line of Necrons advancing on the dock. The last remnants of the Imperial Guard were moving to intercept, but their lasrifles were no match for the Necrons' cannons.

Zelia ducked as a shuttle took off right over her, its boarding ramp only narrowly missing her head. Every ship in the space port was fleeing now. Most made it, but others were struck by Necron energy and sent spinning back to the ground. Others didn't even manage to take off, their hulls dismantled by Necron scarabs before their rockets could fire.

'Mum!' Zelia yelled, looking around. 'Where are you?'

'Zelia!' came the reply as Elise was swept away by the crowd. There was no way they could get to her.

'Erasmus,' Elise shouted, barely able to make herself heard. 'Get the kids onto a ship. Any ship. Just get them away from here.'

'What about you?' Zelia yelled back.

'I'll get to the *Scriptor* and–'

The rest of her sentence was lost in the clamour of the dock. Zelia pushed against the crowd, but Elise was nowhere to be seen.

'Mum? Mum!'

Erasmus grabbed her arm and bundled her forward.

'Wait! What are you doing? We can't leave her.'

The lexmechanic looked her straight in the eye. 'Your mum will be fine. She's a survivor. But she's right – we'll never make it to the *Scriptor*.'

'Then where shall we go?' Mekki asked.

Erasmus pointed to a large voidship that was preparing to depart. 'The *Mercator*. I know her captain. She'll let us on board.'

'Are you sure?' Zelia asked.

Erasmus tapped the leather purse hanging from his belt. 'If she doesn't, I've enough credits to persuade her. Let's go.'

That was easier said than done

as they fought against the tide of spacefarers, all desperate to make their own escape. The servo-sprite led the way, flying high above the heads of the crowd, but by the time they reached the *Mercator*, its cargo doors were closing.

'Quick, get on,' Erasmus yelled, propelling Zelia and Mekki through the closing doors. The voidship rose into the air, and Erasmus leapt, hanging from the bottom of the hatch. He dangled in the air as the *Mercator* swept out of the space port. Zelia and Mekki grabbed his arms and pulled him aboard with seconds to spare. The cargo doors slid shut, all three of them tumbling to the deck.

'Thank you,' he wheezed, trying to get up as the ship was struck by Necron lightning. He tumbled back to the floor, clutching his satchel to his chest. The *Mercator* shook but flew on, seemingly unscathed.

Zelia helped Erasmus up, looking

around for a viewport. 'I need to see if mum took off.'

'Let's find the captain,' Erasmus said, leading them through the crowd. 'Perhaps she'll be able to contact the *Scriptor.*'

They found a stairwell and climbed up to an observation deck. Like the cargo bay, the place was packed, a throng of warm, sticky bodies pressing in from all sides. Zelia pushed forward, sharp elbows jabbing into her as everyone competed for too little space. She didn't know what was more deafening, the relentless bellow of the engines or the frantic jabbering of the frightened refugees. They hadn't even left Targian's atmosphere and arguments were breaking out. The survivors quarrelled, jealously guarding what few possessions they'd managed to bring with them, glaring at each other with suspicion.

And then there was the smell. The place reeked. The stifling temperature on the observation deck was taking its toll. You could almost taste the sweat in the air, stale and bitter.

You could almost taste the fear.

'Zelia, look...' Erasmus pointed towards a large viewport at the far end of the deck. Outside, Rhal Rata was collapsing in on itself, the giant hive tumbling to the ground. A huge cloud of dust billowed up after the *Mercator* as it rocketed away from the surface. All at once, Targian's rust-coloured sky gave way to inky blackness. They were in space. They had got away.

Zelia kept pushing forwards, wanting to see if she could spot the *Scriptor*. The ship jolted, and she staggered, Mekki catching her before she could fall.

That's when she saw the boy, bunched up on the floor by the viewport. It was the ganger who had saved her from a beating on the *Scriptor*. His eyes were wide as he rocked back and forth, arms locked around his knees.

Fighting her way through to him, Zelia reached out her hand to touch his shoulder.

'Hello?'

He jumped, glancing up at her in terror. 'Get away.'

'I wouldn't bother with him,' said a nearby old-timer, sorting tools in a large box. 'He said he was going to help, but he's been a gibbering wreck ever since we took off.'

'So loud,' the boy whined, his voice more like a frightened child than a streetwise ganger. Zelia glanced down and saw Splitter lying by his feet. What had happened to its original owner?

'Zelia, we need to find Captain Klennon,' Erasmus reminded her, but Zelia ignored him. The boy had helped her; now it was her turn to return the favour.

'Have you ever been on a starship before?'

The boy shook his head. 'Never even been off the ground.'

She rested a hand on his arm. The muscles beneath his skin were taut. 'It's all right to be scared.'

He batted her hand away. 'No. No, it's not. If you're scared, you're nothing. If you're scared, you're—'

The ship swayed, and he cried out, grabbing Zelia and pulling her close. This was more help than she'd been prepared to give, but she went with it, trying to push him away as gently as possible. He was muttering beneath his breath.

'Make it stop. Make it stop.'

'It's fine,' she said, quietly. 'Really, it is. Remind me, what's your name?'

'Talen,' he stammered. 'Talen Stormweaver.'

'Pleased to meet you, Talen Stormweaver,' Mekki said politely.

Zelia smiled. 'These are my friends, Mekki and Erasmus.'

'How do you know each other?' Erasmus asked.

'Talen saved me, when the gangers

broke into the ship.'

She turned back to Talen, who had jumped to his feet.

'You said we were safe,' the boy babbled.

'We are now,' she promised.

'Then what are *those*?'

She looked where he was pointing and frowned. The *Mercator* wasn't alone. At least a dozen ships were flying in a loose formation alongside them. Some were Imperial Navy, although most were civilian. However, that wasn't what Talen was looking at.

A flotilla of smaller ships was zooming up from the planet's surface, sleek and powerful, with scythe-like wings glinting in the starlight.

The same ships that had attacked the hive.

'It's the Necrons,' she gasped.

Talen looked at her in confusion. 'Is that what they're called? The aliens?'

She nodded. 'We saw them out in the wastelands. But Space Marines were fighting them. I thought they would win.'

'Then you thought wrong. Look.'

Behind the Necron ships, giant cracks appeared across the surface of Targian. The continents crumbled, light bursting from the ravaged crust. Zelia shielded her eyes as the planet ripped itself apart, exploding into emerald star-fire.

CHAPTER EIGHT

Warp Space

The ship shook as planetary debris buffeted the hull, striking hard against the armourglass viewport. Zelia lurched into Talen, who grabbed her arms to stop her tumbling to the floor.

'Did they do that?'

'The entire planet...' Erasmus whispered. 'Gone,'

The Necron ships kept coming, chasing down the evacuees. Energy lanced from beneath their wings and a battered freighter at the rear of the escaping convoy burst into flames.

The Necrons didn't even stop, screeching through the wreckage to find another target.

The refugees pressed against the viewports as the Necrons tore through one ship after another. How long before those crackling guns turned on the *Mercator*?

'Hey, what are you doing with that?' It was the old man, shouting at Mekki. The Martian boy had a vox-unit in his hands and was probing the device with the haptic implants on his fingers.

'Give it back,' the toolsmith demanded, only to find himself having to fight off an angry servo-sprite. 'It's mine.'

'Here,' said Erasmus, shoving a handful of copper coins into the toolsmith's hands. 'We'll buy it from you. Is that enough?'

'It'll do,' the old man grumbled, counting out the credits in his palm.

The Martian boy thrust the vox into Zelia's hands. She looked at Mekki in confusion, before she heard a familiar voice issuing from the speaker.

'Zelia? Zelia, can you hear me?'

'Mum! Mum, are you all right?'

Elise's voice was distorted by static. *I can't hear you...'* The signal failed, but Mekki reached over and flicked a dial on the side of the vox. Elise was back, faint but recognisable. '*...on the* Scriptor... *Managed to take off before the planet exploded... If I can't find you... meet at... Emperor's Seat... Do you hear me, Zelia... Emperor's Seat...'*

A cry went up behind them. Zelia turned to see a Necron ship right behind them, larger than the rest. Cannons bristled along its wings, their barrels throbbing with the energy that would rip into them at any second.

'Mum...' Zelia yelled into the vox. 'I don't know what you mean. What's the Emperor's Seat?'

The Necron warship prepared to fire, the refugees racing from the viewports as if they could somehow outrun the deadly beams.

'Mum?'

Behind them heavy shutters slammed

down over the viewports, blocking the view of the attacking ship. Zelia felt her stomach flip. That could only mean one thing.

'What's going on?' Talen cried out, looking around in alarm.

'We've gone into warp space,' Zelia told him, willing her guts to stop churning.

'I don't know what that means,' Talen admitted.

'It's a shortcut through another dimension,' Erasmus explained.

'Another dimension?'

'That allows you to cross vast distances in a fraction of the time, yes,' said Erasmus. The voidship shuddered. 'Some journeys are more turbulent than others.'

'What's with the shutters?' Talen said, pressing his hand against the armourglass. 'Why can't we see outside?'

'To look upon the warp is to go mad,' Mekki intoned in his soft, monotonous voice.

'What's that supposed to mean?'

'It means that some things are best left a mystery,' Zelia told him. 'I've no idea what warp space looks like, but if you believe the stories it's a living nightmare.'

Talen gripped his stomach and leaned against the wall. 'I don't feel well.'

'Just hope it isn't warp sickness,' snorted the old toolsmith, still glaring at them.

'W-what's warp sickness?' Talen asked, sweat beading his brow.

'Your head turns inside out,' Mekki told him, 'and your body becomes a puddle on the floor.'

'Mekki!' Zelia scolded him.

'He did ask,' the Martian pointed out.

'They're just stories,' Zelia told him. 'I've travelled all over the Imperium and I've never heard of anyone becoming a puddle.'

'Doesn't mean the stories aren't true,' sneered the toolsmith.

'How come you've travelled?' Talen

asked, turning his back on the old man.

'We're archeotechs,' Erasmus told him. 'We travel from place to place, digging up the past.'

'Why?'

The question seemed to flummox the lexmechanic. 'Why... to learn, of course. To *understand*.'

Talen looked as if the very idea were as alien as the Necrons.

'And that was your mum? On the vox?'

Zelia nodded, looking mournfully at the communicator.

'Can't you get her back?'

'Not while we're in the warp.'

The ship juddered, and then bucked violently, the shutters sliding up to reveal a very different starfield.

'We're not,' Erasmus observed. 'Not any more.'

'What happened?' asked Talen.

Mekki found a cogitator port in the wall and inserted a haptic implant. 'We were thrown back into the materium.'

Talen looked like he was about
to punch someone in frustration.
'The what? Don't any of you speak
normally?'

'We've dropped back into real space,'
Zelia said, checking the vox. 'It
happens, but it's never good. We're
just lucky that the ship is still in one
piece.'

'And that we've escaped the Necrons,'
Erasmus added.

'How do you know? Can't they warp
out or whatever you call it?'

Zelia shrugged. 'To be honest, I don't
know. I think only humans use warp
space.'

'You think? I thought you were the
one who'd travelled from one end of the
galaxy to the other.'

Erasmus cut in. 'Even if that were
possible – which it isn't, by the way –
there's much about aliens that we just
don't know. Not yet, anyway.'

'Until you dig something out of the
ground.'

The lexmechanic beamed at the ganger as if Talen were his favourite pupil. 'Exactly. Until then, the Emperor will protect us.'

'Yeah,' Talen sighed sarcastically. 'Because he's doing such a great job so far!'

'Shhh,' Mekki hissed. 'Someone will hear.'

'So?'

The Martian looked appalled. 'To speak against the Emperor is heresy. He is our Lord and Protector.'

'Yeah, well, I bet he's never had to crawl through a sewer to escape an ambush. Three years I survived beneath the hive, and no one protected me. I had to look after myself.'

Mekki looked confused, as if Talen's statement didn't quite compute. 'You were a member of a gang.'

Talen bristled. 'What of it?'

The Martian arched an eyebrow. 'Then you had protection, from your... compatriots.'

Talen shoved the Martian away. 'You talk like an oldling. Trust me, you still needed to watch your own back, especially in a gang like the Warriors. We were all alone, one way or another.'

Erasmus was peering quizzically at the lad. 'You no longer class yourself one of these Warriors, then?'

'What?'

'You *needed* to watch your back. Past tense. You've left them behind.'

Talen opened up his arms as if to show Erasmus the crowded deck for the first time.

'I don't see them here, do you?' Scowling, he bent down and snatched up the spud-jacker.

Zelia wasn't really listening to the conversation. Instead she was pressing buttons on the vox. The unit was more than a communicator. It seemed to also have data-slate capabilities, although all she wanted to do was re-establish a link to her mum. The servo-sprite fussed around her head, and Zelia swatted it away.

'It only wants to help,' said Mekki, appearing at her side. 'Here, let me.'

He took the vox-slate and started pressing buttons. Zelia turned to the viewport and pulled open her omniscope to search the stars. The captain would soon plunge the voidship back into warp space, maybe after she had made contact with the rest of the evacuation fleet. But where was the *Scriptor*? Where was her mum?

The scope beeped as it locked on to something small in the midst of the pitch-black void. The cogitator automatically zoomed in, but Zelia still couldn't make out what it was. More blips appeared on the heads-up display. Cold dread crept into the pit of her stomach.

Beside her, the vox-slate crackled. A voice hissed from the speakers, but it wasn't her mum.

'Targian fleet... come in please.'

'That's Captain Klennon,' Erasmus

said.

'I appear to have picked up a transmission from the *Mercator*'s flight deck,' Mekki reported.

The voice was bordering on the hysterical.

'We have been thrown out of the immaterium... my Navigator... incapacitated... Please give position... xenos approaching... Repeat. Xenos approaching.'

'Approaching?' Talen echoed. 'What does she mean, xenos approaching?'

Zelia's mouth was dry when she answered. 'The Necrons. They've found us.'

'What?' Erasmus grabbed the omniscope, pulling it from her grip. 'But that's impossible. We must be light years from Targian.'

'Then the Necrons must be capable of faster-than-light travel,' Mekki said, matter-of-factly.

'How can you be so calm?' Talen snapped. Mekki just stared at him.

'Becoming emotional will not help our situation, Talen Stormweaver.'

'Tell that to everyone else,' Zelia said.

Panic had set in on the observation deck, the refugees staring at the advancing fighters in dismay. Some were openly sobbing, while others were gathering up their pitiful belongings as if they had somewhere to run. Even the old toolsmith was pushing through the crowd, wanting to get away from the windows, abandoning all his prized possessions.

'Why have they followed us?' Zelia asked. 'Why are they hunting us down?'

Erasmus looked as though he was going to answer as the ship shuddered violently. The lead Necron ship had fired, green energy flaring around the viewports. A crack appeared in front of Zelia. She watched in strange fascination as tiny fractures started to spread out across the armourglass. How long would it be before the entire window shattered?

Captain Klennon's voice crackled from the vox-slate. '...*under attack... Attempting to jump into the warp...*'

'It's fine. She's going to get us away,' Zelia said, but Erasmus grabbed her arm.

'No. We can't take that risk.' Another bolt struck the ship. 'We need to get to an escape pod.'

'But we'd be thrown out into space,' Talen said, swallowing.

'We'll be alive,' the lexmechanic told him. 'Unless you want to stay here?'

'We *are* more likely to find an escape pod capable of taking three of us,' Mekki pointed out, not trying to be cruel, but simply stating facts.

'No,' Zelia insisted, 'we stick together. Talen comes with us... If he wants to, that is?'

Talen gripped Splitter with both hands. 'I've nowhere else to go.'

'That settles it, then,' Erasmus said, giving Zelia her omniscope. 'Come on.'

Unfortunately, everyone else had had

the same idea. The refugees rushed for the escape pods, scrapping with each other as they tried to scramble into the small lifecraft.

'Here,' Erasmus shouted, pulling open a hatch so the children could enter an empty pod. But before Zelia could clamber into the cramped compartment, a hairy hand grabbed her shoulder, pulling her back.

'*My* pod,' insisted the giant that had all but thrown her into Mekki. It was an Ogryn, a wall of solid muscle with little in the way of brains. Ogryns had evolved on colonies with harsh environments and high gravity. The Imperial Guard often used the brutes as shock troops, but judging by this one's appearance, he hadn't seen service for quite some time. He was missing an arm and his belly had long since given way to blubber.

'Back off, Plank,' Talen said, stepping up to the hulking lout. 'This is our pod. We were here first.'

'And *I* am bigger than you,' the Ogryn grunted. 'So, I say it's mine.'

'We'll see about that,' Talen said, brandishing Splitter.

'Talen, don't,' Zelia told him, before he could get into any more trouble.

The Ogryn's thick lips split into an ugly grin. It wasn't a pretty sight.

'Nice jacker. I'll take that too.' The Ogryn ripped Splitter from Talen's grip.

'Give that back, or you'll be sorry,'

Talen warned.

'Oh yeah?' the Ogryn said, testing the spud-jacker's weight.

'Yeah,' Talen replied. 'Backlash!'

The Ogryn howled as the booby trap was triggered. He crumpled into a heap, electricity surging over his body.

'Get in,' Talen told them.

'What about your weapon?' Erasmus asked as he clambered in through the airlock.

'Leave it. Doesn't look like there will be enough space anyway.'

He was right. The pod was tiny. They barely all fit as they crushed together on the metal benches that lined the escape pod. Mekki plunged his haptic implants into the pod's cogitator, trying to access the launch sequence, his servo-sprite flitting around his head.

There was a growl and the Ogryn appeared at the airlock, screaming.

My pod!

'Shut the door,' Zelia cried out as the giant tried to push his way in.

'I cannot,' Mekki said. 'The abhuman is standing in the way.'

'I don't believe this,' said Talen, undoing the restraining harness he'd already secured across his chest. Grabbing the rail that ran along the low ceiling, he swung forward, his boots thudding into the Ogryn's chest. To everyone's surprise – including Talen – the brute shot back as if fired out of a cannon. There was a beep from the cogitator and the airlock slammed shut, hissing as it sealed.

'Wow,' Zelia said, genuinely impressed.

Talen shrugged as if such things happened all the time. 'Don't know my own strength sometimes.'

'Strap yourself in,' Erasmus said as the ship shook. Through the vox they heard the captain giving the order to jump back into the immaterium. 'We need to launch before they enter the warp,' Erasmus said, 'otherwise...'

'Otherwise what?' Talen asked, snapping his belt back in place.

'Remember what Mekki said. Anyone exposed to the warp goes insane... or worse.'

Talen's voice pitched up another octave. 'What do you mean worse? What's worse than going mad?'

'To be perfectly honest, I don't know,' the lexmechanic admitted. 'And I don't want to find out. Mekki?'

'Almost there,' Mekki said, concentrating on the cogitator.

'Almost isn't good enough,' Zelia snapped.

The captain was counting down to the jump on the vox, the ship coming under wave after wave of Necron fire.

'Five... four... three...'

'Mekki!'

'Two...'

'Now,' barked the Martian. There was a clunk and the escape pod ejected itself into the void at the exact moment the *Mercator* shot into warp space.

Zelia cried out, but her scream was lost in the roar of the voidship's engines. The pod's glow-globes strobed, the walls rattling as they were jettisoned. Had the *Mercator* already leapt into the immaterium? Had they been flung into the nightmarish dimensions of the warp?

Something hard struck Zelia's head, starlight bursting across her vision, and then there was darkness.

CHAPTER NINE

Fleapit

Zelia snapped awake. She had no idea how long she had been unconscious, only that everyone was screaming – including Mekki.

So much for not getting emotional.

The escape pod jolted, throwing her forwards. Only her belt stopped her from crashing into Talen, who was being shaken around like a rag doll in his harness.

They'd hit something – something *hard*. The pod bounced and rolled, turning them over and over.

With one final jarring kick, they came to an abrupt stop, more or less the right way up.

'Is everyone all right?' she gasped.

'Ask me when my head's stopped spinning,' Talen groaned.

Mekki didn't complain. He was already checking the pod's sensors, trying to work out where they had landed.

Zelia pressed the release on her safety belt and winced as the harness whipped away. She could imagine the bruise that was probably already forming where the restraints had cut into her shoulder, not to mention the lump that had sprung up on her head. The deck was littered with boxes and containers from the overhead lockers. She wondered which of those had struck her when they launched.

'Any idea where we are?' Erasmus asked Mekki. The Martian shook his head.

'Nothing is working,' he said flatly. 'Not the pict-feed, not anything.'

His servo-sprite had crawled into an access panel and they could hear it scrabbling around inside the hull, trying to help its master.

Then there was another noise, at the door. It sounded like claws scraping against the airlock.

'What's that?' Talen asked.

'How are we supposed to know?' Zelia replied, staring at the door.

'I just wish you'd brought that weapon of yours,' Erasmus whispered.

'You and me both,' Talen agreed.

The scraping increased. Something was definitely trying to get in.

Talen unclipped his belt and pushed himself up from his seat, stooping against the low ceiling as he faced the door.

'Mekki, open the airlock.'

'Are you crazy?' Zelia asked, the scrabbling becoming more frantic.

'Probably, but I can't see you fighting whatever that is.'

'It could be a wild animal.'

'Then I'd rather face it out there than in here. Mekki – open the doors.'

Mekki's hand went to the controls.

'No,' Zelia shouted. 'We don't know if the atmosphere is breathable!'

But it was too late. With a hiss, the airlock swung open. With a deafening battle cry, Talen launched himself through the open door. There was a flash of orange fur and then the ganger was gone.

Cold air blew into the pod. Outside was a frozen wilderness, snow and ice as far as the eye could see. Zelia scrambled out of the pod, blinking against the glare of an unfamiliar sun.

'Get it off me!' Talen shouted.

The ganger was pinned down in the middle of the ragged path the pod had cut through the snow, a large shaggy animal on his chest.

'By the Golden Throne,' Erasmus exclaimed, following Zelia into the freezing-cold air. 'Is that what I think it is?'

The creature was distinctly ape-like, with matted orange fur and sharp

yellow fangs drawn back in a snarl.
It had bionic implants around its
arms and shoulders, its simian fingers
unnaturally long. Further implants
ran down its spine, armour-like plates
overlapping to form a kind of pack.

'It is a Jokaero,' Mekki said from the
door of the escape pod, his voice filled
with something approaching awe. 'I
have always wanted to see one.'

'We can swap places if you want,'

Talen croaked.

'Please...' Zelia started, stepping towards the ape. 'My friend didn't mean you any harm. We were just scared.' The Jokaero's green eyes darted from her to the others. She turned to Mekki. 'Can it understand me?'

'According to the magos biologis on Mars, the Jokaero are incredibly intelligent. They are master weaponsmiths, capable of understanding the most complex technology.'

'Where did it come from?'

'Does that matter?' Talen gasped.

'I doubt it's from around here,' said Erasmus. He was looking at their surroundings. They'd landed at the foot of a snow-capped mountain, coming to rest on a steep slope. There was a forest full of weird, almost mushroom-like trees to the north and empty plains to the south. 'I think they originated on the Throneworld.'

'On Terra?' Zelia asked. 'Are you sure?'

'Seriously,' Talen grunted. 'Can we do

this *after* you've got it off me?'

Erasmus took a step nearer the creature. 'Did you come from the ship? Did you come from the *Mercator?*'

'How could he?' Zelia asked. 'Surely he couldn't survive a journey through space?'

The ape only growled in response, a deep animalistic sound.

'Can you speak?'

'Who cares?' snapped Talen.

The Jokaero pushed the ganger deeper into the compacted snow.

With a buzz, Mekki's servo-sprite flew from the pod. The snarl fell from the Jokaero's face as it watched the sprite with almost hungry fascination. The tiny robot fluttered down to the ape, settling onto its shoulder, before plunging one of its probe-tipped fingers into one of the Jokaero's implants.

Both the ape and Mekki gasped in unison. Zelia looked to the Martian. His eyes had closed, his head cocked to the side. The ape's head was locked in the same position. Were they communicating?

Mekki's eyes flicked open. 'It belonged to a family in the spires on Rhal Rata.'

'Belonged?' Zelia asked. 'You mean like a pet?'

The Jokaero growled.

'More like a slave,' Mekki told her. 'It... escaped during the attack and got on board the *Mercator*.' He paused, his eyes clouded, as if he was searching memories that weren't his. 'He saw us... getting threatened by the Ogryn... and pulled it away.'

'Ha!' Zelia laughed. 'So much for Talen not knowing his own strength.'

'Oi,' Talen complained beneath the creature.

'He leapt onto the escape pod when we launched, protecting himself from the void,' Mekki continued, his voice cracking. 'He was so scared. So alone.' There was another pause, before Mekki added: 'Flegan-Pala.'

'What's that?' Erasmus asked.

'His name,' Mekki replied. 'His name is Flegan-Pala.'

The Jokaero snorted, nodding in agreement.

'More like Fleapit!' Talen jibed.

The Jokaero jumped off him, glaring at the ganger.

'He does not like you,' Mekki told Talen.

'Tell it the feeling's mutual.'

'I think it knows that already,' Zelia said.

'He...' Mekki corrected her. 'Not it.'

The Jokaero scampered forwards, running on his hands and feet. He swept past Zelia to jump up onto the roof of the escape pod and proceeded to pull chunks of plating from the hull.

'Hey, stop it,' Talen shouted, leaping up.

'No,' Mekki said, raising a hand. 'Wait.'

The Jokaero pulled out a handful of wires and his fingers became a blur as he started to reconnect them in a new configuration. With a sudden thrum of power, light spilled out of the airlock. The Jokaero slapped the roof of the pod, grunting at them in satisfaction.

'He reactivated the powercell,' Mekki gasped as a wave of welcome heat washed out of the escape pod. 'He is a... genius.'

The Jokaero snorted proudly.

'I still think he's a fleapit,' Talen muttered, glaring at the ape.

The Jokaero ignored him, swinging into the pod, where he jumped onto one of the benches and made space for the others.

'I think he wants us to go back in,' Erasmus said.

'Why?' Talen asked. 'So he can beat us to a pulp in comfort?'

'No, because he wants us to keep warm,' Mekki said, clambering back into the pod without hesitation.

'I'm not going in there with that thing,' Talen insisted.

'Then try not to freeze out here,'

Erasmus said, joining Mekki.

Zelia gave Talen what she hoped was an encouraging smile and followed them in. Talen stood and shivered for a moment, his arms wrapped around himself, before giving in.

'Oh, fine – I'll come in. But don't come crying to me if he murders us all!'

CHAPTER TEN

Taking the Lead

Thankfully, all Flegan-Pala did was improve their living conditions. Working with Mekki and the ever-attentive servo-sprite, the Jokaero boosted the internal heaters, until the pod was as toasty as an oven. He then amplified the pod's scry-sensors and linked them to Mekki's wrist-screen.

Unfortunately, the new sensors still couldn't tell them where they were. The stars in the cold sky didn't match any constellation Mekki had stored in his wrist-mounted cogitator. Erasmus suggested that the pod had been ejected at the exact moment the *Mercator* had entered warp space. They might have been slung halfway across the galaxy. It was a miracle that they had survived at all.

Searching beneath the benches, Zelia and Talen found thermo-blankets, which Fleapit fashioned into coats. The Jokaero wasn't exactly happy that Talen's nickname had stuck, but it was certainly easier to pronounce than Flegan-Pala.

They had also found a case of emergency rations, flakes of dried food which Erasmus heated on a hot-plate that Fleapit somehow created from the pod's boosters.

Their first supper on the ice planet was hardly a feast, but it was welcome nonetheless. While Mekki and Fleapit scanned for vox-signals, Zelia braved the elements and ventured outside. Even with her new thermo-coat, the temperature was almost unbearable, but she wanted to take another look at the sky. Staring through her omniscope, she looked from one cluster of stars to another, but there was nothing the scope's primitive cogitator recognised.

'No known constellations,' it reported in her mother's voice.

Zelia sighed. The voice-print was now all she had of her mum. No, that was a lie. Reaching inside her coat she pulled out a crumpled picture. The faded image showed her mum and dad holding a laughing baby. Zelia smiled sadly. That was before her dad had died while excavating a crashed space hulk on Palacos. A tear splashed down onto the pict and froze. Zelia sniffed, slipping the image back into her jacket.

'I'll find you,' she promised her mum out loud.

'Unit not lost,' replied the scope. Zelia laughed.

'Hey!' came a shout from the pod. 'Give that back!'

She rushed back inside to find Mekki sprawled across the floor, Talen standing over him. How was that even possible? There hadn't been enough space to swing a gyrinx before. How was the pod now large enough for Talen and Mekki to fight?

'What's going on?' she asked.

Talen was holding the leather pouch he usually kept on his belt.

'Your friend is a thief,' Talen spat.

Fleapit jumped between them, stretching out a long arm to protect Mekki.

'I was not stealing,' the Martian insisted. 'I only wanted to see if it contained something that could help construct a beacon, to send out a distress signal.

'There's nothing for you in there,' Talen said, snapping the pouch back onto his belt.

Zelia looked at Erasmus, who just shrugged, holding his own satchel close.

'Don't look at me. They're old enough to sort out their own disagreements.'

Zelia threw up her hands in exasperation. 'Thanks, Erasmus, that's a great help.'

'Don't take it out on him,' Talen said. 'He's right. What's it got to do with you, anyway?'

Zelia couldn't believe what she was hearing. 'What's it got to do with us? Talen, if we're going to survive all this, we're going to have to try to get on with each other.'

'Why? We're not friends.' He jabbed a finger at Mekki. 'He didn't even want me here.'

'Can you blame me?' Mekki muttered, just loud enough for them to hear.

'Mekki!' Zelia exclaimed.

'No, it's fine,' Talen said. 'I get it, Cog-Boy. I'll stay out of your way, if you keep out of mine.'

'But Talen—' Zelia began, only for the ganger to cut her off.

'No, Zelia. I don't need him, and I don't need you. I don't need anyone.'

There was a buzz and a glowing hololith appeared in the air, projected from one of the lenses Mekki wore around his head. It showed Talen, back on the voidship, grabbing Zelia and holding her close. Talen stared at it in horror, especially as the hologram zoomed in to focus on his terrified face.

'*Make it stop,*' the hololith pleaded. '*Make it stop.*'

'Mekki, that's enough!' Zelia shouted.

The electronic image vanished, although Mekki still glared at a visibly shocked Talen.

'What was that?' the ganger stammered.

'Mekki keeps a holo-log of our expeditions,' Zelia explained, 'recording everything we discover.'

'That doesn't mean he can record me,' Talen said, going to stomp outside.

Zelia tried to stop him. 'Where are you going?'

'Anywhere he isn't,' said Talen, shooting a venomous look at the Martian.

Zelia let him pass. The door swung open and, after a sudden gust of wind, slammed shut.

She dropped onto one of the benches, suddenly feeling bone-tired. She looked up at Mekki, who was frantically tapping on his wrist-display to hide his anger.

Day one, and they'd already come to blows. Mekki and Talen were arguing, and then there was Erasmus. She'd expected the lexmechanic to take control, but he had retreated into himself, content to sit in the corner of

the escape pod hugging that satchel of his.

Someone had to take the lead, and it looked like it was going to be her.

'So, Mekki,' she said, forcing a smile, 'tell me about this beacon...'

CHAPTER ELEVEN

Searching for Scrap

Humans were fools. Flegan-Pala had always known this, of course he had, and he hadn't seen anything to change his mind since crashing on this frozen rock.

He'd wanted to clear them out of the escape pod before it had launched from the voidship, but dealing with that dunderhead of an Ogryn had meant the door had slammed shut before he could finish the job. Instead, he had had to crawl into a service hatch barely larger than himself, enduring the entire journey with his long arms wrapped around his body. Still, he was used to surviving in cramped surroundings. He'd spent enough years being locked in the dark with no space to move.

Since they had landed, the stupid bipeds hadn't stopped arguing, even the Martian youth, who seemed more intelligent than most. At least Mekki could understand him and didn't refer to him by that ridiculous nickname.

The first night had been long, with few of them able to sleep. Flegan-Pala had expanded the internal dimensions of the escape-pod to make them all more comfortable, but no one even seemed to notice, not even Mekki.

Only the mindless servo-sprite seemed to fully appreciate his work. In fact, it wouldn't leave him alone. Flegan-Pala wondered if it wanted to be augmented. He could easily arm it with a few digi-weapons. Maybe mount some thunder-missiles on those little wings or give the little flitter an electro-sting... The Jokaero made a mental note to conjure something up for the mechanical imp at some point in the future.

Of course, for that they'd need supplies. Like all of his race, Flegan-Pala could create the most sophisticated machines from the most basic parts. That's what made him such a valuable slave. He scratched at the restraining implant that had been fitted around his neck. It was the only device he couldn't tamper with, not unless he wanted a thousand volts surging through his nervous system. Still, his master was now half a galaxy away. There was no way he could activate the implant from that distance, thank the Old Ones. Flegan-Pala was safe here, whatever the conditions.

But even his genius had limits. Flegan-Pala had done much with the pod, but needed fresh material. Otherwise he'd have to start cannibalising the sprite, or maybe the girl's omniscope. And then there was whatever the ruffian was hiding in his pouch. The young oaf had slept hugging it last night. Still, Flegan-Pala knew the importance of secrets. He didn't want the others to know about his own secret stash either. That was for emergencies.

Flegan-Pala shivered through his fur. He despised the cold, almost as much as he despised this sorry bunch of refugees. Still, they were being useful now, all except for the one the others called Erasmus. The older human had refused to join the trek out into the forest to look for any components that may have fallen from the escape pod during its descent, anything they could use to make Mekki's distress beacon. He'd just turned his back on them, practically curled up on one of the benches, muttering beneath his breath: 'It will all be all right. It will be all right.'

Something was obviously wrong with the oldling. Perhaps the destruction of Targian had derailed what was left of his fragile human mind, not that the children seemed to have noticed.

Flegan-Pala shook his head. He had lived in the presence of humans for centuries, passed from master to master like the possession he had become, and yet the Jokaero still couldn't fathom how Terrans had ever conquered the stars. They were primitive and selfish, afraid of everything that was not like themselves, convinced of their own superiority. They moved through the galaxy like a virus, a disease, infecting everything they touched... But for now he needed them, even though they disgusted him.

He could already feel his joints stiffening with the cold. If he was forced to withdraw into a hibernation-cycle he would need the humans to maintain the camp until they were rescued. *If* they were rescued. He needed to construct the beacon first.

His foot touched something beneath the snow. It was a shard of dark red metal. Flegan-Pala's brow furrowed. That hadn't come from the pod. He sniffed the scrap, and then licked it, the biometric sensors in his tongue delivering a full report of its atomic structure to the cogitator embedded in his brain. It was of human manufacture, at least originally. Flegan-Pala's hair bristled. Humans had been to this planet before. Interesting…

Something moved through the trees – if indeed you could call them trees. They had mottled stalks rather than trunks, and wide caps instead of foliage. How had the girl described them when the group had set off this morning? Giant mushrooms. Flegan-Pala wondered if they could be used in some way or another. The prospect of constructing an organic weapon appealed to him.

There it was again, moving between the stalks. One of the younglings, perhaps? No. It was too tall. The adult, then? Had he finally pulled himself out of his sulk?

Flegan-Pala whistled through his teeth, and the servo-sprite came flying. It landed on his open palm and allowed him to access the tiny control point between its wings. Usually Flegan-Pala would create a swarm of spy-flies, but there was no need with the servo-sprite already here. Linking the sprite to his own optical implants, he let the robot fly off again, seeing through its tiny eyes. His heart raced in his chest and for a moment Flegan-Pala was lost in the exhilaration of swooping through the air. Such freedom was as alien to him as the humans who had kept him locked in the darkness for decades at a time, but it made his soul sing in a way he had never dreamed possible.

The sprite buzzed over Talen and the girl, both searching for salvage in the snow. Flegan-Pala sniffed. They had found little that even he could use to build a distress beacon. At this rate, he'd definitely have to ransack his own reserves. That was… annoying.

Putting his frustrations aside, he urged the sprite on, searching for whoever it was that he'd spotted between the trees.

Yes. There was definitely someone else in the forest. There were marks in the snow, deep footprints. Flegan-Pala shifted uncomfortably. Judging by the length of the strides, whatever had made them was taller than any of the humans. The sprite flew faster,

sweeping between the stalks, but then stopped sharply, Flegan-Pala's jaw dropping open as he realised what the sprite had been tracking.

The figure was tall, with heavy armour across its broad shoulders and a single glowing eye in the middle of a silver skull. It stalked through the wood, a large rifle clutched in its skeletal hands.

There was a Necron on the ice planet, and not just any Necron – a *Hunter*.

He had thought they were safe here, but he was wrong. Maybe he was as foolish as the humans.

The Necron had come for them, and this time there would be nowhere to hide.

CHAPTER TWELVE

Cover Your Ears

Zelia looked up as something charged towards them.

'What's that?' Talen said, putting himself in front of her.

'Let me see,' she said, shoving him aside. For a guy who wanted to be left alone, he spent a lot of time trying to protect her.

A flailing shape came barrelling out of the mushroom-trees, kicking snow everywhere. Zelia went to run, until she realised it was Fleapit.

The Jokaero was thrashing his long arms in the air and screeching at the top of his lungs, the servo-sprite following close behind.

'What is it?' she asked as the simian floundered towards them. 'What have you found?'

The Jokaero chattered an agitated response, but she was forced to shake her head. 'I can't understand you.'

'Where's Cog-Boy?' Talen asked. 'He can talk to this thing.'

'You mean Mekki,' she corrected him. 'And I don't know.'

The Jokaero rolled his eyes and grunted at the servo-sprite. The robot darted obediently into the trees, reappearing a few moments later with a panting Mekki.

'The sprite said there was danger,' the Martian gasped.

Fleapit chattered at him and Mekki raised his hands. 'Slow down, please. You're talking too fast.'

The Jokaero growled in frustration and flexed his shoulders. As the children watched in amazement, the metal plates on his back opened like

doors and the servo-sprite flew inside.
Mekki went to look where it had
gone, but Fleapit raised a warning
hand. Seconds later the servo-sprite
emerged carrying a ridiculous amount
of technology, which it dumped into
the snow. The doors slammed shut and
Fleapit turned his back on them to
rummage through the pile of gadgets.

'Where did that lot come from?' Talen
asked.

Mekki could only scratch his bald
head in puzzlement. 'I have heard
that Jokaero hide secret supplies of
technology as rodents store nuts for
winter.'

'Hide them where? In thin air?'

'Something like that,' Mekki replied.
'In micro-dimensions.'

Talen looked at Zelia for support. 'Do
you understand any of this?'

She nodded, watching Fleapit work.
'I think so. Erasmus has talked about
them in the past. Micro-dimensions are
supposed to be pocket universes, much

smaller than our own.'

Talen shook his head. 'Nope, that doesn't help at all.'

'Think of them like the warp,' Mekki said, picking up the explanation. 'A miniaturised reality that theoretically can be accessed by a portal or gate.'

'You mean that thing on his back?' Talen asked as Fleapit started to bolt the gadgets together. 'It's like a magic door where he keeps his stuff?'

'Not magic,' Mekki insisted. 'Science.'

'Same difference,' Talen said, although a smile spread across his face as he realised what the Jokaero was building. 'It's a cannon! A dirty, big cannon!'

He was right. Fleapit's jumble of gadgetry had been transformed into a large firearm that the Jokaero gleefully hefted onto his shoulder.

'But why would we need a cannon?' Zelia asked.

No one had a chance to answer as a bolt of green energy sizzled through the air between them to smash into one of the trees. The children dived for cover as the giant mushroom crashed into the clearing.

There was no mistaking that energy.

Talen looked around in panic. 'Was that... was that a *Necron*?'

Fleapit babbled an unintelligible reply before aiming his cannon.

'Cover your ears!' Mekki warned, and the Jokaero fired.

The cannon didn't fire energy or plasma bolts. Instead a beam of pure sound shrieked into the trees, striking the nearest stalk. The tree shattered into a thousand icy pieces, its cap crashing down to the ground.

'Wow!' Talen cheered as the snow settled. 'That was *amazing*.'

Zelia's ears were still ringing. 'You can't be serious.'

'Are you kidding me?' Talen laughed, turning to the Jokaero. 'Fire it again!'

Fleapit didn't need telling twice. He squeezed the trigger and another deafening shriek sliced through the trees in front of them.

'It is a sonic cannon,' Mekki said, his face almost breaking into a grin.

'Fighting with sound?' Talen asked. 'That I've got to see!'

Fleapit chattered a response that no one but Mekki could understand.

'He says he saw a Necron Hunter in the forest. It is searching for us.'

'Then I want a sonic cannon!'

'No,' Zelia snapped. 'No more weapons.'

Talen's eyebrows shot out. 'Why not?'

'Because we don't need them.'

More lightning fizzed out of the trees. They threw themselves to the ground as Fleapit returned fire.

'You sure about that?' Talen asked.

'It's like mum always says,' she said, trying to reason with him. 'We spend our lives digging up wargear. Weapons, tanks, old armour, not to mention the bones of the people who used them. We should learn from the mistakes of the past, not make them all over again.'

'Tell that to the Necron!' Talen yelled.

Another mushroom-tree exploded in a blaze of green energy.

'Where is it?' Mekki asked, peering into the trees.

'Who cares?' Talen replied, grabbing Zelia's hand. 'We need to get to cover.'

Zelia yanked her hand free but ran all the same. They dived between the stalks as Fleapit unleashed a fresh salvo of sonic pulses. Zelia looked back and realised that the Jokaero was giggling. He was actually enjoying himself.

He was going to get them all killed.

Another of the giant mushrooms came crashing down. She yelped and rolled out of the way. She looked up, spitting snow from her mouth. Where were Talen and Mekki? Had they got out of the way of the great tree, or been crushed beneath its stalk?

Something moved behind her, a flash of dull silver among the mottled trees. Zelia clapped a hand over her mouth to stop herself from screaming. It was the Necron, rifle in hand. She ducked behind the nearest mushroom-tree, only daring to peek out once her heart had stopped hammering. The alien was gone. Then she saw it again to her left, stalking away from her. How had it moved so fast?

She wanted to warn the others but knew shouting would give away her position. She needn't have worried. Spotting the metal skeleton, Fleapit turned and fired, obliterating even more trees. Zelia was thrown back, thermo-coat flapping. When she looked up again, the Necron was gone.

Had it been buried?

'Zelia, behind you!'

She snapped around, startled by Talen's shout. The Necron was racing towards her, a rictus grin beneath its glowing eye. She turned and ran, imagining a wave of green lightning washing over her, but skidded to a halt when she saw another Necron straight ahead. Its weapon was raised and ready to fire.

CHAPTER THIRTEEN

The Sound of Victory

'Get down!'

Zelia didn't know who shouted the warning, Talen or Mekki, but she followed it all the same. She dropped into the snow as Fleapit swept his cannon in a wide arc, sonic energy slicing through all the trees like a knife.

She was sure the forest was going to come crashing down on her, but miraculously she survived the devastation. She looked up to see Talen running at full pelt, the Necron lurching after him.

As she watched in terror, the skeletal

stalker shimmered and vanished, only
to reappear in front of the fleeing
ganger. It shot out a grasping hand,
but Talen ducked, dropping into a
roll. The Necron's gaunt fingers closed ·
around thin air, and then it was gone
again. Talen scrabbled to his feet and
started to run towards her, when the
air behind him started to shimmer.

Zelia jumped up, knocking Talen to
the ground as Necron energy zapped
over their heads. By the time they
looked up, wiping snow from their eyes,
the Necron was nowhere to be seen.

Talen jumped to his feet. 'They're
everywhere.'

'No,' she told him, 'I don't think
there's more than one. It's the same
Necron, not an entire army.'

'But how can it move so quickly.'

'I think it can teleport.'

'Teleport? How?'

She shrugged. 'I don't know. Magic?'

Talen helped her up. 'Don't let Mekki
hear you saying that.'

She brushed snow from her cape. 'What if it can slip in and out of our dimension like a voidship coming out of warp space?'

'Or Fleapit's pocket universe.'

'Exactly. It just looks like it's everywhere at once because it's hopping from place to place.'

Someone barged into them. Talen reacted instinctively, grabbing the newcomer and throwing them over his shoulder.

'Ow,' Mekki groaned from where he had landed in the snow.

'Talen!' Zelia scolded, helping Mekki back to his feet.

'Sorry,' Talen said, looking suitably embarrassed. 'I thought you were skull-features.'

Mekki straightened his lenses. 'The Necron is phasing through real space—'

'Yeah,' Talen cut in. 'Hopping from dimension to dimension to confuse us.'

Mekki looked shocked, and maybe even a little disappointed that they had worked it out for themselves. 'Well, yes. But I cannot get Flegan-Pala to listen. He has gone berserk.'

That much was obvious by the constant scream of the sonic cannon.

'But there's no way the monkey will hit the Necron if it can flit in and out of reality,' Talen said.

'First of all,' sniffed Mekki, 'Flegan-Pala is a Jokaero, not a monkey.'

'Does that matter?'

'Yes,' Mekki insisted, 'but we can argue about that later. In the meantime, you are right. It is extremely doubtful that Flegan-Pala will score a direct hit.'

'You don't say,' Zelia said, pulling Mekki out of the way of another beam.

'I do, however, have a plan.'

'Well, don't keep us in suspense,' Talen snapped.

'I set the sprite on reconnaissance mode,' Mekki told them. 'It noticed that the Necron froze for a fraction of a second whenever the sonic beam swept near.'

'Froze?'

'As if the pulse interfered with its systems in some way. Flegan-Pala may be a terrible shot, but at least his weapon appears to disorientate our enemy.'

'But even if the monk—' Talen sighed as Mekki shot him a dark look. 'Even if the *Jokaero* manages a direct hit, I've seen Necrons in action. Blast 'em to pieces and they just pull themselves back together.'

'Then blasting is not the correct course of action.'

'Do you have any other suggestions?' Zelia asked, just as the Necron shimmered into view beside them. She cried out as its fingers clamped around her arm, Fleapit snapping around to focus on her scream. He fired, the sonic bolt hitting the Necron square in the chest. The alien's body shattered, and Zelia was thrown clear. She landed

in a heap, but even then wasn't safe.
The Necron's severed hand was still
locked around her wrist, its cold fingers
twitching. She shook it loose and it
thudded to the ground.

Talen was beside her so fast she
almost wondered if he had learnt how
to teleport too. 'Are you hurt?'

'I'm fine,' she said, staring at the
creepy hand. It was moving, crawling

back towards the Necron's fragmented body.

Talen lunged forward, and Zelia realised that he was going for the Necron's discarded gun.

'No,' she said, pulling him back. 'No weapons, remember?'

'That's your rule, not mine,' he snapped back, before his eyes went wide and he shoved her out of the way of a bolt of Necron lightning.

The Necron's other hand was still curled around the rifle's trigger. Even when it wasn't connected to a body, those skeletal fingers still wanted to destroy them.

But the hand wouldn't stay disconnected for long. Talen was right. The scattered parts of the Necron were already knitting back together. With a cry of frustration, Zelia kicked out, booting the rifle so it was aiming away from them. The Necron's skull chattered, the eerie sound disturbingly like a laugh. It was staring past her, and Zelia felt the hairs bristle on the back of her neck. She threw herself down as another blast of sonic energy rushed over her, nearly taking off her head.

'This is ridiculous,' Zelia spluttered. 'If the Necron doesn't get us, Fleapit will.'

'I will stop him,' Mekki said, spotting that Fleapit had his back to them and was firing indiscriminately in the other direction. Before Zelia could stop him, Mekki ran into the clearing, dropping to the ground as Fleapit spun around to unleash another volley.

'Flegan-Pala... it is I, your friend, Mekki.'

The ape stopped, panting hard, his eyes wild and unfocused.

Zelia glanced back and saw that the Necron had almost reformed. Soon it would be able to snatch up its cannon and finish them off once and for all. Grabbing Talen's hand, she dragged him towards the others, where Mekki was talking Fleapit down.

'It is not going to work, Flegan-Pala,' the Martian was saying. 'The Necron can self-repair, but I think we can disrupt its systems if we move quickly.'

'*Really* quickly,' Zelia urged them. 'It's almost back together. What are you thinking, Mekki?'

Mekki reached out for Fleapit's cannon. 'May I?'

The ape snatched it away, glaring at the boy.

'You can trust me,' Mekki insisted. 'We are a team. We work together.'

Fleapit glared at the children, but reluctantly let Mekki take the sonic gun. The Martian sagged under its weight, but Talen stepped forward, helping him carry it behind the shelter of a fallen mushroom-tree.

Zelia could hear the Necron's joints popping back into place across the clearing.

'Whatever you're going to do, you need to do it now.'

Mekki was already at work, his haptic implants connected to the cannon. He was reconfiguring components on the weapon's barrel with his other hand, sliding parts back and forth.

Fleapit's eyes went wide as he realised what the Martian was doing, and he let out an eager grunt. He dropped to Mekki's side and started to assist.

Mekki looked into the Jokaero's excited face. 'It should work, yes?'

'What should work?' Talen asked. 'What are you doing?'

Something fizzed in the trees behind them. The Necron had teleported again. Zelia looked around, wondering where it would reappear. The answer came in a bolt of green energy, streaking from behind. Fleapit pulled her down, squealing as the lightning glanced off his long arm. He snatched it back, a black streak across his forearm where the ray had scorched the orange hair. Fleapit's teeth were clenched against the pain, but he was still alive. They had been lucky, but there was no telling how long their luck would hold.

The Necron shimmered into being on the other side of the fallen tree. It stood tall, weapon raised, barely a scratch on its metal chest.

The snow crunched beneath its metal feet as it marched towards them.

'Mekki,' Zelia hissed through gritted teeth.

The Martian slapped the last component in place. The sonic cannon was a mess, cables running everywhere, but Mekki seemed happy with his work.

'This might hurt,' he warned them, slamming his hand onto a switch he'd fashioned from the trigger.

Zelia gasped with pain as an electronic banshee wail burst from the mangled cannon. The noise was unbearable, a long, high-pitched howl that seemed to cut through her bones.

'We need to go.' It was Mekki, shouting right into her ear, struggling to be heard above the cannon's scream. 'The pulse won't last much longer.'

He helped her up, and she fought the urge to be sick. The sound was churning her stomach, her vision blurring as she staggered to her feet. She could barely put one foot in front of the other, but if it was hurting her, it was doing a lot worse to the Necron.

The alien had collapsed into the snow, its body jerking uncontrollably as if thousands of volts were surging through its body. Its glowing eye flickered in time with the pulse, smoke rising from its servos.

The Necron wasn't the only thing affected by the noise. Mekki's sprite was convulsing on the floor, overwhelmed by the sonic attack. The Martian scooped it up and made for the trees, Fleapit lolloping in his wake. She teetered after them, forcing herself to run, only dimly aware of Talen racing alongside.

The Necron didn't lurch after them. It

was too busy screaming silently at the sky. Its ridged spine arched, its skeletal body bending in two. Then, with a sudden flash of light, it vanished into thin air.

They had won... for now.

CHAPTER FOURTEEN

The Truth

'Do you think we destroyed it?' Talen asked as they made their way out of the mushroom forest.

'You're the one who said it was indestructible,' Zelia reminded him. 'I expect it's disappeared back to wherever it came from to lick its wounds.'

The shriek of the sonic pulse still echoed around the frozen landscape, drawing a worrying rumble from the top of the snow-capped mountain. If Mekki's device caused an avalanche, their escape pod would be buried, with Erasmus still inside.

Without warning, the noise cut out.

'The powercells must have died,'
Mekki said, puffing as they clambered
up the slope to the escape pod. Fleapit
muttered something, and Mekki nodded.
'We can recover them later to use
for the beacon. Of course, if you had
mentioned you had a secret supply of
technology...'

Fleapit grumbled as the accusation
was left hanging in the chilly air.

Erasmus was already outside as they
reached the pod. 'What was that awful
noise?' he said, shivering in his shirt
sleeves.

Talen looked like he was going to
knock the old man to the ground. 'Oh,
sorry, did it wake you up?'

'Talen...' Zelia warned, before he lost
his temper.

'No, it's fine. I mean, it's not like we
were being attacked by a Necron while
he was tucked up nice and warm.'

Erasmus's face went as white as the
snow beneath their feet. 'A Necron?
Here?'

'We'll explain once we're inside,' Zelia said. 'It's freezing.'

And explain they did, shut inside the pod, each cupping a beaker of boiled water in their hands.

'I'm so sorry,' Erasmus said, when they'd finished their tale.

Talen wasn't about to forgive him that easily. 'That we were nearly killed, or that you weren't there to help us?'

Erasmus didn't say anything but rested his hand on the satchel beside him. Talen eyed it suspiciously.

'Just what have you got in there?'

'In what?' Erasmus asked innocently.

'In your bag.'

'It's none of your business.'

Talen jumped up to confront the lexmechanic. 'You're hiding something.'

Now Erasmus was also on his feet, jabbing a finger at Talen. 'Says the tunnel-rat who wouldn't let us look in his precious pouch.'

'This isn't about me,' Talen said, clenching his fists. 'But call me that one more time and I'll show you *exactly* what a tunnel-rat can do.'

'Stop it, both of you!' Zelia shouted, nearly throwing her beaker across the pod, anything to shut them up.

Erasmus was the first to back down. 'I'm sorry, it's just...'

He turned to look down at the bench. His satchel was gone.

'Where is it?' he shouted, dropping on his knees to look beneath the seat.

'Is that what you're looking for?' asked Talen, pointing at Fleapit, who was hanging upside down from the rail on the ceiling, Erasmus's satchel in his hands.

'Give it back,' Erasmus yelled, swiping at the ape, but Fleapit thrust his hand into the bag and pulled out a large hoop made of tarnished metal.

'What's that?' Talen asked as Fleapit flipped down to the floor. The Jokaero turned the hoop over in his hands, eyes glittering with fascination. Zelia felt something, but it wasn't fascination. It was disgust.

The hoop looked big enough to be worn as a headdress and was covered in strange alien glyphs... the same symbols she'd seen emblazoned on the wings of the Scythe-like fighters that had attacked Rhal Rata.

'Is that... Necron?' Erasmus tried to grab the metal artefact, only for Talen to block him. 'I don't think so.'

'Please,' the lexmechanic begged. 'Please, be careful with it.'

Zelia held out her hand to Fleapit. 'Can I see?'

The Jokaero glared at her, holding the hoop close to his hairy chest. He glanced at Mekki, who nodded. The ape huffed and handed it over.

Zelia couldn't suppress a shudder as she took hold of the strange object. The metal felt unnaturally cold in her hand, exactly like the Necron Hunter's grip on her wrist. She ran her fingers along the symbols carved into the dull surface.

'Where did you get it?'

Erasmus sank down onto the bench.
'I... I found it at the dig, buried in the
ground.'

'Back on Targian?'

He nodded, ashamed.

Mekki frowned. 'I did not see it in the
catalogue.'

Erasmus shook his head. 'I didn't tell
Elise. I... recognised the markings.'

'You knew what it was?' Zelia asked.

'Where it had come from?'

He looked up with pleading eyes.
'Do you know how rare it is to find
Necron artefacts? When Necrons die,
their bodies vanish. When I saw the
markings, I thought... I thought...'
His voice cracked, tears running down
stubble-strewn cheeks.

'You thought it would make you rich,'
Talen said.

'No,' Erasmus insisted, wiping his nose
with the back of his hand. 'I thought
I could take it to one of the institutes
on Terra, perhaps even the Scholastica
Xenosa on Teleos. I thought if I brought
them something like this, they might
offer me a place in their chambers, that
I could study in a librarium...'

'Rather than scrabbling around in the
dirt,' said Talen.

'But you didn't tell mum,' Zelia said,
her voice bitter.

'She would have told me to submit it
to the Inquisition or destroy it.'

'Because she knew it was dangerous.'

'It's just a relic,' he insisted. 'A piece of jewellery, like a crown or coronet.'

'Do the Necrons look like they wear crowns?'

Talen's eyes widened as he realised the truth. 'That's why they attacked the hive. That's why they came to Targian.'

'We don't know that,' the lexmechanic said quickly.

'Oh, it's a coincidence is it? You dig up some Necron junk on a dust bowl in the middle of nowhere, and all of a sudden, the Necrons themselves decide to pay a visit...'

'They were looking for this,' Zelia said, remembering the Necron fighters carving up the wasteland.

'Or whatever else was under the ground,' suggested Mekki.

'And you brought it with you?' yelled Talen. 'They came after the ships. They came after us.'

'It's just a relic,' Erasmus repeated, mournfully.

Talen wasn't about to let this go. 'If

it's just a relic, then it wouldn't have been of interest to your institutes or libraries. If it's just a relic, the Necrons wouldn't have destroyed Targian, they wouldn't have blown up all those ships or sent a Hunter after us.' He jabbed a finger at the coronet. 'Everyone would still be alive.'

'I'm sorry,' Erasmus sobbed. 'If I had known...'

'You *should* have known,' Talen yelled. 'You're supposed to be the clever one. I didn't have much of a home, but it was where I belonged. And now it's gone. Onak, the Warriors...' His voice cracked with emotion. 'Even my mum and dad... I may have hated them, but they didn't deserve that. None of us did. And all because you took that thing...'

He lunged at Erasmus, and the lexmechanic recoiled, throwing up his arms. Mekki and Fleapit dived after Talen, holding him back.

'It's your fault,' Talen screamed. 'All your fault.'

'Talen, stop it,' Zelia told him. 'Stop it.'

The ganger broke free of the others' grip, but stayed where he was, his hands still bunched into fists as he glared at Erasmus. 'All your fault.'

'So,' Mekki asked, his voice as calm as Talen's was choked with fury, 'what do we do now?'

'We destroy it,' the ganger replied.

Zelia tested the hoop's strength. 'I doubt that's even possible, especially if it's made from the same metal as the Hunter.'

'Then we throw it away,' Talen said. 'Chuck it into a crevasse or something.'

'And what if the Necron finds it?'

'Then it'll leave us alone. Everyone wins.'

'Really?' Zelia couldn't agree with that. 'If what you say is true, if the Necrons came to Targian looking for this crown, if they ripped the planet apart...'

'It must be dangerous,' Erasmus said, his voice haunted with guilt.

'What if this is part of a weapon,' she asked, 'or something worse?'

'Worse?' Talen snorted at her. 'I thought you believed *nothing* was worse than a weapon...'

'I do, but who knows what this thing could do in the wrong hands. In *Necron* hands.'

Talen threw out his arms in exasperation. 'Then we're doomed, aren't we? We can't destroy it and we can't throw it away. And if we keep it, then good news – the Hunter will just keep coming.'

'Not if we fight back.'

Everyone looked at Erasmus.

'What?' Talen scoffed. 'Have you lost your mind? You didn't see it! It's unstoppable.'

'You stopped it, didn't you? With Mekki's sonic pulse.'

'We have no way of knowing if it was destroyed,' Mekki pointed out.

'Yes,' the lexmechanic agreed, 'but what you said about the way it hopped in and out of real space...'

'What about it?' asked Talen.

'Why didn't it just attack?'

'It did!' Talen insisted.

'No, not at first. What if it was toying with you, trying to work out if you had the crown before striking?' He stood up, a fresh gleam in his eyes. 'But it's not the only thing that can play tricks.'

'What are you talking about?' Talen said, as the lexmechanic looked around the pod and found the ration case. The children watched in bewilderment as he turned out the tiny packs of dried food onto the bench and held the empty case out to Zelia. It was just big enough for the crown.

She hesitated and then placed it inside. Erasmus thanked her and snapped it shut.

'Now what?' she asked.

'Now we get to work.' Erasmus turned to Mekki and Fleapit. 'The sound-machine you built from the sonic cannon... Do you think you could make some more?'

CHAPTER FIFTEEN

The Relic's Call

The Necron flexed its clawed fingers.
The servos in its hands were still
working, the effects of the sonic attack
now passed. Outwardly, the Hunter
stood strong in the safety of its ship,
but inwardly it seethed.

It knew little of organics, other than
how to kill them, yet was aware of
enough of their biology to know that
the three fleshlings were nothing more
than infants. It had been beaten by
children. *Children!*

The indignity burned in its core.

The Hunter vowed that it would make
them suffer, once it had recovered the

Diadem of Transference, of course. That was its primary objective: locate and obtain the Diadem.

Only then could it have its revenge.

Stalking through to the armoury, the Hunter accessed his weapons. The tesla carbine had proved less than satisfying. The Hunter reached out and plucked a disintegrator from its place on the rack before drawing a hyperphase sword that had extinguished the life force of thousands of targets in its long service. The Necron still had no idea which of the humans was hiding the Diadem. The crown remained silent, refusing to respond to the Necrons' call. Nothing about this made sense. The Diadem had been thought lost, but then had been heard across the stars. Its cry had roused the warriors of the Ketatrix in their stasis-crypts, but then had fallen silent. The Astromancer had tracked its call to an insignificant planetoid the humans called Targian. The Ketatrix Nightfleet had reduced the blighted world to rubble, but the Diadem had vanished.

The Hunter was just one of a number of Deathmarks despatched by Overlord Merlek to track Targian's few remaining survivors, but it was determined that it would be the one to return the Diadem to the tomb world. It would personally deliver the relic into Merlek's hands. The time for games had passed. The disintegrator couldn't harm the artefact. If one of the children was hiding the Diadem in the folds of their ridiculous coats, the Hunter would simply atomise them, bones and all, revealing the relic for all to see.

Priming the weapon, the Hunter slipped into hyperspace, leaving its ship far behind. Leaping from hyperspace to the ice planet and back again, the Necron flashed towards the infants' last known location, covering incredible distances with each bound.

Before long it was back in the forest. Night had fallen, the planet's sun dropping beneath the horizon. The forest was as silent as a tomb. With a click of its head, the Hunter activated its internal sensors, searching for advanced technology. The humans must have a ship nearby, a shuttle or some kind of raft. Find that, and the Necron would find its prize.

Yes. There it was – a signal nearby, on the mountainside.

It had them now.

It leapt through hyperspace, appearing on a snowy plain at the foot of a rocky crag. It ducked behind a boulder, gazing across the frozen waste. There was a camp, huddled beneath more of the strange trees, a primitive hut sheltering against the wind.

No, the Hunter realised. Not a hut. A life raft, from the organics' spaceship. The humans had erected a perimeter, the air shimmering between tall poles. A sonic fence. Foolish fleshlings. As if that would protect them.

The Necron shifted forward, appearing

inside the humming barrier. The pod was open, snow blowing into the hatch, but the Hunter could see from here that it was empty. It looked around. There were canvas tents dotted around the camp, flimsy structures that would offer little protection against the cold. The Hunter cocked its head. It could hear something. Whispered voices, coming from the farthest tent.

'This will never work, Zelia.'

'Erasmus said it would.'

'"Erasmus said. Erasmus said." This is the same Erasmus that lied through his teeth, yeah? This is all his fault. He brought the Necron artefact here.'

The Diadem! The Hunter raised its disintegrator and fired. The tent dissolved in an instant. The Necron rushed to the patch of melted snow. There was no sign of the relic.

'Did you hear that? Was that a weapon?'

The Necron whirled around. The voices had moved. They were behind him now.

'Keep quiet, Talen.'

The Hunter fired again, systematically destroying each and every tent in turn. Still there was no sign of the relic.

'Get away from here. Now!'

Another voice. Deeper. Older. The Hunter spun around to face its foe.

A squad of Space Marines stood in front of it, their gleaming blue armour etched with the scars of a thousand battles. But something was wrong. Why did they not raise their chainswords and attack? Why waste time on words, when battle would reveal their true purpose?

It was a mistake the Emperor's playthings would learn to regret.

The Hunter opened fire, the emerald beam slicing through the nearest warrior's chest-plate.

The Space Marine shimmered but remained standing. The Necron swept its weapon along the line of warriors, cutting through the sentinels one by one.

'Get away from here. Now!'

The Necron ceased its attack. The disintegrator beam had left no marks on the Emperor's warriors. They stood like statues, bolters and chainswords in hand, but still didn't attack.

The Necron drew its sword and swept it through the two nearest Space Marines, expecting the vibrating blade to cleave through the fleshborn's power armour.

It passed through the warriors both, but where was the shriek of Necron

steel against ceramite? The sword slipped through the organics as if they were ghosts.

The Necron engaged its sensors, searching for the power source it already knew had to be hidden nearby. There, beneath the immobile Space Marine's boot. The Hunter plunged its hand through its enemy's foot, finding the holo-projector buried in the snow. It crushed the tiny blue lens in its palm, and the Space Marines wavered before vanishing completely.

They had not been real. They were hololiths.

The Hunter paced over to the escape pod, its sensors finding another projector wedged into a rock. The Hunter brought its sword down on the device and the escape pod disappeared.

It was all a trick. A deception.

'I tell you, this isn't going to work. We can't fight that thing.'

The Hunter marched towards the last remaining tent and thrust its hand through the shelter's holographic side. It pulled out a data-slate containing a vox. A small flying robot shot out of the fake tent, taking to the air. It had been dragging the transmitter around the camp, playing with the Hunter, treating it like a fool. No more. The Necron reached up, grabbing the machine in its fist, and crushed the automaton before it could escape. Twisted mesh wings tumbled to the snow.

'Please, Talen,' a female voice said from the vox. 'You need to be quiet. The Necron will find us.'

Yes, the Hunter promised. Yes, I will.

On the other side of the mountain, Zelia and the others huddled in the open hatch of the real escape pod. Zelia and Talen talked into the vox on her sleeve, their voices transmitting to the slate the Hunter now held in its hand. Mekki had created the decoy using his holo-projectors but had remained unconvinced of Erasmus's plan. They all had – but Erasmus had been proved right. The plan was working. They just needed to manoeuvre the Hunter over the sonic mine they had hidden in the snow beneath the fake camp.

'So what if he finds us?' Talen yelled into the vox, starting to *really* overact. 'That Necron isn't so scary. I could open him up like a tin of sludge-beans.'

Zelia rolled her eyes at him, and was about to respond, when Mekki cut in.

'The servo-sprite. It has gone.'

'What do you mean, gone?' Zelia asked.

The Martian was staring down at his wrist-screen. 'The data-stream has been terminated. The sprite is offline.'

They couldn't wait any longer. Zelia turned to the Jokaero. 'Fleapit, detonate the sonic mine.'

Inside the pod, the ape grinned and thumbed a button. Zelia waited for a shrill whine to erupt from the other side of the mountain. They had it all planned. The sonic mine would set off an avalanche, disorientating the Necron long enough for it to be buried deep beneath the snow before it had a chance to escape.

But there was no whine and no rumble from the mountain.

'Try again,' she told the Jokaero.

The button clicked and clicked as Fleapit repeatedly jabbed at it, becoming increasingly frustrated, but still nothing happened.

A voice hissed from the pod's speakers, an eerie, unnatural rasp like nails against plastek.

Your plan has failed, fleshborn, your sonic device crushed beneath my foot. And now, I shall do the same to you.

The vox-link went dead.

Talen leapt up. 'It didn't work. The Hunter's coming for us.'

'We can still stop it,' Zelia insisted.

'With what?'

They turned to the Martian. 'Mekki, how many sonic mines did you construct?'

'Two,' Mekki told her. 'But we can make more.'

'By the time it gets here?' Talen said. He darted into the escape pod.

'What are you doing?' Zelia asked.

Talen pushed Fleapit out of the way and started ransacking the inside of the escape pod.

'Giving the Necron what it wants. I don't care if it's a weapon or not. If the Necron wants the crown, it can have the crown.'

Zelia jumped in after him. 'You can't.'

'Watch me.' Talen dropped onto his knees to look under the bench. 'Where have you stashed it, Erasmus?' He looked up from his search. 'Erasmus?'

There was no answer. Zelia realised she hadn't seen the lexmechanic for a while.

'Where did he go?' she asked Mekki.

The Martian shrugged. 'He said he was going to keep watch.'

*I'm afraid that was a lie.'

'Erasmus?' The lexmechanic's voice

had come from her vox. Zelia talked urgently into her sleeve. 'Erasmus, where are you?'

CHAPTER SIXTEEN

Facing the Enemy

On the south face of the mountain, Erasmus hugged the ration case to his chest. The wind cut through his cape, chilling him to the bone as he talked into his vox.

'It's going to be all right, Zelia. Everything is going to be just fine.'

'What are you doing?'

Erasmus smiled. She sounded so like her mother.

'I'm putting things right. As I should have done on Targian.' With a flourish, he held the ration case above his head, shouting out across the snowy plain.

'I have what you're looking for,' he

shouted, his voice echoing back at him. 'It's here.'

'You've taken the coronet?' Zelia spluttered over the vox.

'I have the case,' he confirmed.

The wind was whistling around the mountain now, whipping up snow. A storm was coming.

'What are you waiting for?' he bellowed.

A shadow appeared in the snow. Erasmus could make out its angular body, sharp lines illuminated by the dull green of its disintegrator cannon and glowing eye.

'There you are,' he said, snowflakes clinging to the stubble on his chin. 'What took you so long?'

'He's gone mad,' Talen said. 'The idiot's going to get himself killed.'

'You were the one who wanted to hand over the crown,' Zelia reminded him, pulling on her coat.

'Where are you going?'

She made for the exit. 'To stop him. We can't let the relic fall back into Necron hands, not after everything that's happened.'

'It is not going to,' said Mekki, looking past her. Zelia turned to see Fleapit holding the crown in his hands as he silently communicated with the Martian.

'Where did you find that?' Talen asked.

'It appears that Erasmus had Flegan-Pala store it in a micro-dimension,' Mekki explained.

'But if the crown is here,' Zelia said, 'what has Erasmus got in the case?'

The spectral light of the disintegrator glowed all the brighter as it swung up to face Erasmus. The lexmechanic smiled. He was scared, of course he was, but at last he was making amends.

'Don't you want to see it?' he asked the alien, trying to disguise the fear in his voice. 'After all, you've been through a lot to find it.'

'The Diadem,' the Necron hissed. 'Give it to me.'

'The Diadem, eh? Is that what it's called? Fascinating. But I think you're going to be disappointed.'

Erasmus threw the case in front of the Hunter, its lid flipping open as it hit the ground. The Necron's eye pulsed with anger.

Mekki's second sonic mine was nestled at the bottom of the case.

'Get the Diadem to Elise,' Erasmus shouted to Zelia over the vox, as he activated the detonator hidden in his pocket. 'She'll know what to do with it.'

The mine's scream echoed around the mountainside. The Necron staggered back, and Erasmus clutched his ears as the mountain itself seemed to growl.

Erasmus looked up to see a tidal wave of snow rushing towards them, rocks and trees carried down the mountain in its wake.

He leapt forward, shoving the pained
Hunter into the path of a rolling
boulder. It was like trying to topple a
statue.

The shriek of the mine was drowned
by the roar of the avalanche, and
Erasmus's world turned white.

'Erasmus? Erasmus, are you there?
Please come in.'

Zelia's voice cracked as she screamed

the same question over and over again. The roar of the avalanche had drowned out the mine, and Talen ran outside to make sure that they weren't about to be buried themselves.

Gradually, the night stilled, the last echoes of the landslide fading to nothing.

Zelia activated the vox and asked again, desperate to hear Erasmus's voice. Yes, he had lied to them. Yes, he had put them all in danger, but that didn't mean that she didn't care about him. He was her friend, and now he was gone.

'Erasmus... *please...*'

A hand touched her shoulder.

'Zelia...'

She turned, half expecting to see Erasmus's lop-sided smile or the spectacles permanently perched on top of his head.

But it was only Talen, hesitating, not really knowing how to cope with her grief.

Zelia buried her head in the ganger's chest and let the tears flow.

CHAPTER SEVENTEEN

A New Dawn

Talen had left camp early the next morning, saying he was going to check to see if there was any sign of the Necron. A flurry of fresh snow had fallen overnight, covering all traces of the avalanche. Zelia found the ganger sitting on a rock, looking out over the mushroom forest.

'Find anything?' she asked.

He shook his head, playing with the clasp of his leather pouch.

'What *do* you keep in there?' Zelia asked, sitting beside him.

He ignored the question, and she backtracked quickly. 'I mean, if you don't want to show me, that's fine. I just wondered...'

Talen passed the pouch to her. She took it, strangely nervous as she popped open the clasp.

Inside was a small wooden toy – a Guardsman, its lasrifle aimed at an unknown enemy.

'My brother gave it to me,' Talen told her, 'before he enlisted. Told me to keep it safe, to remind me of him.' He smiled sadly. 'As if I could forget.'

She turned the toy over in her hands, before replacing it carefully in the pouch. 'Enlisted? He was an Imperial Guardsman?'

'Just like my dad, and his dad before him. A family of soldiers...'

She clicked the clasp shut. 'But not you.'

'No. Not me. Let's just say I had other ideas.' He took the pouch back and attached it to his belt. 'Didn't want to end up fighting heretics and...' He suppressed a laugh.

'And aliens?' she prompted with a knowing smile. 'How's that going for you?'

He returned her grin. 'Funny you should ask...'

Zelia pulled out her omniscope, snapping it open.

'Activating,' the cogitator announced in her mother's voice.

'Guess we both carry reminders of people we love,' she said.

'But your mum's still out there.'

She frowned at him. 'You mean... your brother...?'

He shrugged. 'We never heard from him again. Dad always said he was out there somewhere, serving the Emperor, but I know he's gone...' Talen tapped his chest. 'In here.'

She didn't know what to say, so settled on a simple: 'I'm sorry.'

Talen pushed himself from the rock, brushing snow from his coat.

'So, you're determined to do this, then?' he said, changing the subject. 'To take the Diadem to your mum.'

Zelia let him help her up. 'If we can find her, yeah.'

'First things first, we need to get off this planet,' Talen pointed out. 'Any ideas how we're going to do that?'

'Actually, yeah,' she replied with another smile. 'One or two...'

They trudged back to the escape pod to find that Fleapit had worked more of his techno-miracles. The pod itself looked even bigger, as if the Jokaero had somehow stretched it. He'd also constructed a series of posts around the camp, a real sonic fence which activated with a hum as soon as Zelia and Talen walked into the circle.

They headed over to Mekki, who was putting the finishing touches to a tall mast topped by a glow-globe.

'You've finished your beacon,' Talen said.

'With a little help from a friend,' Mekki said, looking up as a servo-sprite buzzed down from the pulsing red lamp.

'I thought that thing was destroyed.'

'So did Mekki,' Zelia told him. 'Fleapit made him a new one before they started work.'

She reached out to stroke the Jokaero's head, but the ape swatted her hand away, baring his teeth.

'Fine,' she said, quickly. 'Hint taken. No petting.'

'The beacon is transmitting a distress signal on all known Imperial channels,' Mekki told them as the sprite landed on his shoulder.

Zelia nudged Talen in the ribs. 'See? We'll be off this planet before you know it. Someone's bound to pick up our signal, sooner or later.'

'Yeah,' said Talen, shielding his eyes as he looked up at the flashing light, 'but how do we know it'll be the right someone?'

In the grand halls of the Inquisition, a

pair of intense eyes snapped open. The man had been meditating, his devotions interrupted by a small light flashing on the stone altar that dominated his chamber.

He rose from his knees, and walked to the altar, pressing a button set into the stone.

A hololith appeared above the granite slab, a star map with a single light pulsing in the darkness.

The Imperium had received hundreds of distress calls since the fall of

Targian – thousands – but there was something about this one, something that called to him across the stars.

This one felt different.

This one felt *important*.

Could it be the Emperor himself, guiding his hand? Had his prayers finally been answered?

A servo-skull whirred up beside him, offering assistance, but he waved it away. He needed to concentrate. He reached into the hololithic image, opening his fingers so it zoomed into a small cluster of stars.

Yes... It was there. He could *feel* it, in his very soul.

'There's no need to worry, whoever you are,' he said aloud, his voice deep and commanding. 'Salvation is on its way.'

The servo-skull reappeared, carrying a long coat in its metal tentacles. The man smiled, the skin beneath his mask crinkling.

'How well you know me, Corlak.' He pulled on the coat with a flourish, straightening the immaculate cuffs. 'Prepare my ship. We have a new mission... A *rescue* mission.'

Slipping his force sword into its scabbard, Inquisitor Jeremias strode purposely from his chambers.

GALACTIC COMPENDIUM

PART ONE

THE IMPERIUM OF THE FAR FUTURE

Life in the 41st millennium is hard.
Ruled by the Emperor of Mankind
from his Golden Throne on Terra,
humans have spread across the galaxy,
inhabiting millions of planets. They
have achieved so much, from space
travel to robotics, and yet billions
live in fear. The universe seems a
dangerous place, teeming with alien
horrors and dark powers. But it is also
a place bristling with adventure and
wonder, where battles are won and
heroes are forged.

ZELIA

Twelve-year-old Zelia is the daughter
of galactic explorer Elise Lor. She grew
up helping Elise with archaeological
expeditions on dozens of worlds, digging
up ancient artefacts and alien technology.
Bright and resourceful, Zelia always thinks
she knows best, but isn't as experienced
as she tries to make out.
Sharing her
mum's hatred
of weaponry, Zelia
believes that the best
way to overcome fear
is to learn about the
universe. That doesn't stop
her from being terrified
of spiders, having been
trapped in the web of a
gigantic temple-weaver when
she was a small child.

MEKKI

Like all Martians, Mekki is happiest when
tinkering with technology, and is able to
communicate with the machine-spirits
that dwell inside vehicles and cogitators.
A talented inventor, eleven-year-old Mekki
created the special robotic frame that
supports his paralysed arm as well
as servo-sprites, a swarm of tiny
robot helpers. Even though
they grew up together,
Mekki and Zelia have
never been close. Mekki
prefers the company of
machines to humans
and often finds it hard
to make friends. He
can be incredibly
tough on himself,
especially when
things go wrong.

DID YOU KNOW?
Only one person knows why Mekki
really left Mars – Zelia's mother, Elise.

TALEN

The son of a loyal Imperial Guard officer, thirteen-year-old Talen ran away from home to avoid being enlisted in the military. He fell in with the Runak Warriors, a feral gang who lived in the tunnels beneath Rhal Rata, the largest hive city on Targian. Used to thinking with his fists, Talen finds it difficult to trust anyone, but has a good heart. Once he is on your side, you couldn't ask for a better friend. Talen has little experience of the galaxy, hiding his insecurities beneath bluster and bravado. His only link to the past is the toy soldier his older brother gave him before going off to war, a treasure he will guard with his life.

SPACE MARINES

Sworn defenders of humanity, Space Marines are the ultimate warriors, graced with superhuman speed, strength and stamina. Genetically engineered to fight in the countless wars of the 41st millennium, these towering giants have two hearts, three lungs and blood that is immune to all known poisons. Organised into Chapters, the Emperor's chainsword- wielding champions are feared and respected throughout the galaxy. Bravest of all are the heroic Ultramarines. Clad in blue-and-white power armour, they plunge into battle, risking all to protect the Imperium against aliens and the forces of Chaos.

DID YOU KNOW?

Potential Space Marine recruits are gathered at an early age from all across the Imperium. If they survive the selection trials, they then must endure years of training and genetic engineering. Once this process is completed, they have been transformed into super-soldiers who defend mankind from any threat.

NECRONS

Long ago, the galaxy lived in terror of the sinister Necrons. According to legend, these evil tyrants transplanted their twisted minds into bodies of living metal, creating immortal armies of indestructible skeletal warriors. The Necrons enslaved thousands of worlds, but were eventually defeated, forced to place themselves in suspended animation for millions of years. Now, they are rising from their secret tombs, led by fearsome Overlords, ready to reclaim the universe they once ruled. In battle their sickle-winged space-fighters scream through the sky while swarms of cybernetic scarabs devour any metal in their path. Have no doubt, the Necrons are unfeeling and unstoppable.

NECRON WEAPONS

Hyperphase Sword –
with a blade that vibrates so fast it can slice through anything.

Gauss Weapons –
energy weapons that disintegrate an enemy atom by atom.

Death Ray –
can vaporise tanks or even carve through the armoured walls of a hive.

Tesla Cannons –
capable of melting a Space Marine's power armour.

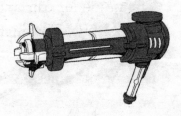

DOOM SCYTHE

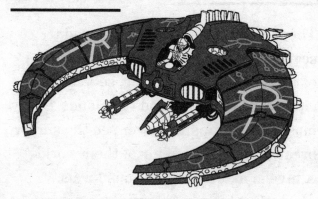

Vehicle type:	Necron fighter aircraft
Dynastic Markings:	The Ketatrix Dynasty
Pilot:	Necron warrior
Weapons:	Death Ray, Twin-linked Tesla Destructor

COGITATORS

The name for computers in the 41st Millennium. The Tech-Priests of Mars believe that each cogitator contains a 'machine spirit', although no cogitator is allowed to develop self-awareness. Artificial or 'Abominable' Intelligence is seen as dangerous and must be destroyed on sight.

HIVE WORLDS

There are thousands of hive worlds
scattered across the Imperium. Billions
of citizens live in towering, self-contained
cities that reach beyond the clouds. Sadly,
most hive occupants never see the sun or
breathe the polluted air of their world.
A hive is made up of various levels:

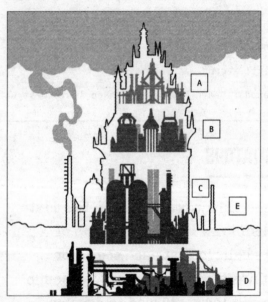

DID YOU KNOW?
Terra is a super-hive world, the entire globe
covered by one sprawling city. Millennia
ago, the planet was called Earth.

A   **The Spires** – Where the richest and the most powerful citizens live in luxury. Life in the 41st millennium doesn't get much better than this. Unless the Necrons send the entire hive crashing to the ground, of course.

B   **The Upperhive** – home to the nobles, bureaucrats and manufactorum- owners who rule the colossal cities in the Emperor's name.

C   **The Lowerhive** – Most of the population lives in the lowerhive, scratching a meagre existence in filthy manufactorums. Every day is a grind, with barely any food and no respite from toil. Lowerhivers live to work, nothing more.

D   **The Underhive** – If you thought life in the lowerhive was tough, nothing will prepare you for the underhive. Home to the poorest citizens, every day is a fight to survive. Vicious gangs rule the labyrinthine tunnels and sewers, locked in a never-ending turf war.

E   **The Outskirts** – Only the bravest or most desperate souls choose to live in the poisonous wastes that surround the hive. Dangerous animals stalk the toxic landscape where no crops can grow.

ABOUT THE AUTHOR

Cavan Scott has written for such popular franchises as *Star Wars, Doctor Who, Judge Dredd. LEGO DC Super Heroes, Penguins of Madagascar, Adventure Time* and many, many more. The writer of a number of novellas and short stories set within the *Warhammer 40,000* universe, including the *Warhammer Adventures: Warped Galaxies* series, Cavan became a UK number one bestseller with his 2016 World Book Day title, *Star Wars: Adventures in Wild Space – The Escape*. Find him online at www.cavanscott.com.

ABOUT THE ARTISTS

Cole Marchetti is an illustrator and concept artist from California. When he isn't sitting in front of the computer, he enjoys hiking and plein air painting. This is his first project working with Games Workshop.

Magnus Norén is a freelance illustrator and concept artist living in Sweden. His favourite subjects are fantasy and mythology, and when he isn't drawing or painting, he likes to read, watch movies and play computer games with his girlfriend.

WARHAMMER
ADVENTURES
STORIES FROM THE FAR FUTURE

WARPED GALAXIES

An Extract from book two
Claws of the Genestealer
by Cavan Scott
(out May 2019)

The forest was silent. A fresh blanket of snow had fallen overnight, drifting through the gaps of the strange mushroom-trees. No birds whirled above their wide frozen caps, or insects crawled along their mottled stalks.

Heat had no place here. At night anyone caught outside without protection would freeze, and conditions barely improved during the day.

A snout pushed out of the snow. A small, pot-bellied creature scrabbled from its burrow. The tiny ridge-boar, barely a month old, shook snow from its milky-white spines. It snorted, its breath misting in front of stubby tusks. The boarlet looked around, its eyes becoming accustomed to the glare of the surface. It lifted its blunt nose into the chilly air and sniffed once... twice...

Satisfied that no predators lay in wait, the young creature trotted deeper into the forest. It didn't care about the snow, or the tracks it left in its wake. All it cared about was the gnawing hunger in its belly.

It struggled on, the trot becoming a scramble, the boar's skinny legs disappearing into the snow-drift. Every now and then it stopped, churning up the snow with its snout, searching in vain for roots or berries. The snow was too thick, the ground too hard.

Its nose twitched. There was a scent, something new. The boar darted forwards. There, in the middle of a clearing, a pile of dried flakes lay piled on a stump. The boar crept forwards cautiously, sniffing the air. The smell of the food made its belly rumble. The animal pounced upon the unexpected feast, grinding the flakes between its teeth. They tasted so good.

Unfortunately, they were also a trap.

A net flashed through the air. The ridge-boar squealed, kicking up snow as it scampered away. The net missed its target, landing on the stump. The boar disappeared between the frozen stalks, and a nearby voice cursed.

Talen Stormweaver stepped out from his hiding place and grunted in frustration. He had been so close that time. If only he'd been quicker springing the trap. With a sigh, he snatched up the net he'd woven from voidship cables, shaking loose the excess snow. At least the hunt hadn't been a complete waste of time, not like yesterday or the day before. This time he'd actually found something.

This time he had tracks to follow.

Trying to tread quietly, Talen followed the hoof-marks in the snow. Two weeks they'd been on this Throne-forsaken planet. Two weeks. He still wasn't used to the cold. Yes, he was wrapped in a thick thermal coat, but the chill was relentless. He'd almost forgotten what it was like to be warm.

Talen wasn't used to this. Home was the tunnels beneath Rhal Rata, the largest hive on Targian. It was never cold beneath the great city. It was wet and dark and stank so bad your eyes watered, but you were never in danger of freezing to death. You could be attacked by another gang or find yourself facing dire-cats in the crawlways, but you were always warm. Plus, food was everywhere, even if most of it didn't belong to you. There were stalls ripe for looting in the markets above and plump sewer-rats fresh for hunting in the tunnels below.

Here, there was nothing.

No, that wasn't exactly true. There was a ridge-boar. He just had to find it again.

Of course, his home wasn't there anymore. There had been times when he'd loathed life on Targian, but now the planet was gone forever. The entire hive world had been torn apart by the Necrons, living alien machines. Talen had escaped the destruction, more by luck than by judgement, and had ended up on this ice-box with a ragbag bunch of survivors. There was Erasmus, a stuffy old lexmechanic, and Zelia, one of the bossiest girls he'd ever met. They were the normal ones. The rest of the group was made up of Mekki, a Martian kid who was happier dealing with machines than humans, Fleapit, an orange-furred Jokaero with a knack for making weapons out of next to nothing, and a tiny winged robot called a servo-sprite. It was Fleapit who had fashioned the thermo-coats, and who had somehow transformed their cramped escape pod into a shelter large enough to house all six of them.

No, Talen corrected himself. Not six. Not anymore.

A Necron Hunter had followed them to the ice planet, searching for an ancient artefact the old man had been hiding – the Diadem. They had barely survived with their lives, and only because Erasmus had made the ultimate sacrifice. The archeotech had lured the Hunter into the path of an avalanche. Both were buried beneath tonnes of snow on the other side of the mountain.

At least, they *hoped* the Hunter was buried. Talen had seen those skeletal horrors in action, seen them repair themselves in the heat of battle. They could also leap from place to place, phasing in and out of real space. Every night, Talen dreamed of steel skeletons clawing their way out of icy tombs, or appearing above his bed, green eyes blazing.

Zelia told him he was being paranoid. 'The fact that we're still breathing proves that it's destroyed,' she'd told him. 'Or at least damaged beyond repair. It's gone. We're safe.'

The Diadem itself was now stashed in Mekki's backpack, shielded by a gizmo that the Martian had made from a vox-caster. It would stop other Necrons from finding it, at least that's what Zelia said.

Zelia said a lot of things. She and the others were content to sit in the shelter, huddled near the distress beacon Mekki and Fleapit had erected, waiting to be rescued. Not Talen. The escape pod's emergency rations were almost exhausted. Someone had to find more food, and it might as well be him.

Besides, no one was coming to help. The beacon had pulsed for two weeks with no answer. It was time to face facts. They were stranded.

Talen crept through the towering stalks, wincing as his boots crunched in the snow. He didn't want to scare the animal any more than he already had. There it was, floundering in the snow ahead. The boar was caught in some kind of root, unable to get away. The more it thrashed, the more entangled it became. Finally, a stroke of luck!

Talen grinned. 'Hello, lunch!'

Talen rushed forwards, throwing his home-made net over the creature. The boar squealed, extending its spines to protect itself.

'Shut up, will you?' Talen complained, as he pulled the net tight, the boar trussed safely inside. It writhed and screamed but had no way to escape. 'How can something so small make so much noise?'

There was another snort, over to his left. Talen looked and saw another ridge-boar glaring at him. While the one in his net was an infant, this one was fully-grown, spikes bristling along its arched back. It glared at Talen, head down, large pointed tusks jutting forwards.

'Nice piggy,' said Talen, raising what he hoped was a calming hand. 'Nothing to see here. Go on. Shoo.'

With a ferocious bellow, the angry boar charged straight for him. Talen let go of the net and ran for his life.

'Help!' he screamed, although no one could hear him. The boar was almost on him, grunting as it carved a path through the snow.

Talen's muscles burned with the effort of running through the thick snow. He pelted forwards, and then cried out in alarm as the ground disappeared beneath him.

He fell, tumbling through thin air, before landing with a bone-jarring crunch far below. Snow tumbled down from above. The boar had stopped itself from following Talen over the edge. It snuffled around the hole that had opened beneath his feet. Talen groaned, clutching his arm as the animal gave up on its revenge and scooted away.

Talen tried to sit up, and pain lanced through his shoulder. He couldn't move his arm. Was it broken?

Breathing hard, he looked around at his new surroundings. Icy walls rose high on either side of him. He had no hope of climbing them with one arm. He pushed himself up to a sitting position, trying not to pass out with the pain, and stared into the gloom of the cave. Were those passages in the shadows? Had he tumbled into a labyrinth? He was used to navigating tunnels, but at least he had known where he was going back on Targian. He had no way of knowing where these icy passages led. One false move and he could stumble into an even bigger drop.

Grimacing, he reached into his coat,

searching for his vox. Fleapit had fashioned small communicators for each of them, and Talen prayed that his hadn't been damaged in the fall. He pulled it out of his vest. The case was cracked, but hopefully it would still work.

'Hello?' he croaked, opening a channel. 'Can you hear me? Zelia? Mekki? Anyone?'

There was no answer. He shook the box and tried again. Someone would answer, sooner or later.

They just had to...